*Stories of Horses
and Their Riders*

GENTLE LIKE
A CYCLONE

Stories of Horses
and Their Riders
GENTLE LIKE
A CYCLONE

Selected by

Phyllis R. Fenner

Illustrated by Lorence Bjorklund

William Morrow and Company

New York · 1974

Copyright © 1974 by Phyllis R. Fenner

Grateful acknowledgment is made for permission to reprint the following:

"That Mark Horse" and "Jeremy Rodock" by Jack Schaefer. From the book *The Plainsman*, Copyright 1952, 1953, 1954, 1956 by Jack Schaefer. Reprinted by permission of Houghton Mifflin Company.

"Blood Royal" by Montgomery M. Atwater. Originally published in *St. Nicholas Magazine*. Used with permission of the author and his agents, Lenniger Literary Agency, Inc., 437 Fifth Avenue, New York, N.Y. 10016.

"Breakneck Hill" by Esther Forbes. Reprinted by permission of the American Antiquarian Society.

"Chiltipiquín" by William Brandon. Copyright 1943 by The Curtis Publishing Company. Copyright renewed 1970 by William Brandon. Originally published in *The Saturday Evening Post*. Reprinted by permission of Harold Ober Associates Incorporated.

"Throw Your Heart Over" by Stuart Cloete. Copyright © 1960 by Stuart Cloete. Originally published in *Ladies Home Journal*. Reprinted by permission of John Cushman Associates, Inc.

"Last Bronc" by Colin Lofting. Copyright © 1954 by The Curtis Publishing Company. Originally published in *The Saturday Evening Post*. Reprinted with permission from *The Saturday Evening Post*.

"Lanko's White Mare" by H. E. Bates. From the book *Seven Tales and Alexander* by H. E. Bates, Copyright 1930, Copyright © renewed 1958 by H. E. Bates. Reprinted by permission of the Viking Press, Inc.

Printed in the United States of America.

1 2 3 4 5 78 77 76 75 74

Library of Congress Cataloging in Publication Data

Fenner, Phyllis Reid (date) comp.
    Gentle like a cyclone.

    CONTENTS: Schaefer, J. That Mark horse—Atwater, M. M. Blood royal.—Forbes, E. Breakneck hill. [etc.]
    1. Horses—Legends and stories. [1. Horses-—Fiction]
I. Bjorklund, Lorence F., illus. II. Title.
PZ10.3.F38Ge   [Fic]   74-2499
ISBN 0-688-21821-0
ISBN 0-688-31821-5 (lib. bdg.)

A WORLD FAMOUS HORSE STORY LIBRARY Selection

CONTENTS

For Ola and Jimmy Glenn,
whom I dearly love.

HORSE SENSE

There are many good reasons to give one's heart to a horse. He has qualities we admire. He is loyal, responds to affection, can be trained to do our bidding. And, according to legend, the horse is the wisest of animals. "Horse sense" is still a common expression.

Whether an aging mare or a wild stallion, horses appeal to old and young, men and women. Although we live in a horseless-carriage age today, the horse is more popular and loved than ever.

P.F.

THAT MARK HORSE
Jack Schaefer

Not that horse, Mister. Not that big slab-sided brute. Take any or all of the rest, I'm selling the whole string. But not that one. By rights I should. He's no damn good to me. The best horse either one of us'll likely ever see, and he's no damn good to me. Or me to him. But I'll not sell him. . . .

Try something, Mister. Speak to him. The name's Mark. . . . There. See how his ears came up? See how he swung to check you and what you were doing? The way any horse would. Any horse that likes living and knows his name. But did you notice how he wouldn't look at me? Used to perk those ears and swing that head whenever he heard my voice. Not anymore. Knows I'm talking about

him right now and won't look at me. Almost ten months
it is, and he still won't look at me. . . .

That horse and I were five-six years younger when this
all began. I was working at one of the dude ranches and
filling in at the rodeos roundabout. A little riding, a little
roping. Not too good, just enough to place once in a
while. I was in town one day for the mail, and the post-
master poked his head out to chuckle some and say there
was something for me at the station a mite too big for
the box. I went down and the agent wasn't there. I scouted
around and he was out by the stock corral, and a bunch of
other men too, all leaning on the fence and looking over.
I pushed up by the agent, and there was that horse inside.
He was alone in there, and he was the damndest horse I'd
ever seen. Like the rest around I'd been raised on cow
ponies, and this thing looked big as the side of a barn to
me and awkward as hell. He'd just been let down the chute
from a boxcar on the siding. There were bits of straw
clinging to him, and he stood still with head up testing the
air. For that first moment he looked like a kid's crazy
drawing of a horse oversized and exaggerated with legs
too long and big stretched-out barrel and high-humped
withers and long-reaching neck.

The men were joshing and wondering was it an ele-
phant or a giraffe and I was agreeing, and then I saw that
horse move. He took a few steps walking and flowed forward into a trot. That's the only way to put it. He flowed
forward the way water rolls down a hill. His muscles
didn't bunch and jump under his hide. They slid easy and
smooth, and those long legs reached for distance without
seeming to try. He made a double circuit of the corral with-

out slowing, checking everything as he went by. He wasn't trying to find a way out. He just wanted to move some and see where he was and what was doing roundabout. He saw us along the fence, and we could have been posts for all the particular attention he paid us. He stopped by the far fence and stood looking over it, and now I'd seen him move there wasn't anything awkward about him. He was big and he was rough-built, but he wasn't awkward anymore even standing there still. Nobody was saying a word. Everyone there knew horses and they'd seen what I saw. "Damn it to eternal hell," I said. "That's a horse."

The agent turned and saw who it was. "Glad you think so," he said. "It's your horse. This came along too." And he stuck a note in my hand.

It had my name on it all right. It was from a New York State man who ran some sort of factory there, made shoes I think he told me once. He'd been a regular at the ranch, not for any dude doings but once a summer for a camping trip, and I'd been assigned to him several years running. It wasn't long. It said the doctors had been carving him some and told him he couldn't ride again so he was closing his stable. He'd sold his other stock but thought this horse Mark ought to be out where there was more room than there was back east. Wanted me to take him and treat him right.

I shoved that note in a pocket and eased through the fence. "Mark," I called, and across the corral those ears perked stiff and that big head swung my way. "Mark," I called him again and that horse turned and came about halfway and stood with head high, looking me over. I picked a coil of rope off a post and shook out a loop, and he watched me with ears forward and head a bit to one side. I eased close and sudden I snaked up the loop and it was open right for his head and he just wasn't there. He was thirty feet to the left, and I'd have sworn he made it in one leap.

Maybe a dozen times I tried, and I didn't have a chance. The comments coming from the fence line weren't improving my temper any. Then I noticed he wasn't watching me, he was watching the rope, and I had an attack of common sense. He was wearing a halter. This wasn't any Western range horse. This was one of those big Eastern crossbreds with a lot of Thoroughbred in them I'd heard about. Likely he'd never had a rope thrown at him before. I tossed the rope over by the fence and walked toward him, and he stood blowing his nostrils a bit and looking at me. I stopped a few feet away and didn't even try to reach for the halter. He looked at me and he was really seeing me the way a horse can and I was somebody who knew his name out here where he'd been dumped out of the darkness of a boxcar. He stretched that long neck and sniffed at my shirt, and I took hold of the halter and that was all there was to it. . . .

That was the beginning of my education. Yes, Mister, it was me had to be taught, not that horse. The next lesson came the first time I tried to ride him. I was thinking what a big brute he was and what a lot of power was penned in him and I'd have to control all that, so I used a Spanish spade bit that would be wicked if used rough. He didn't want to take it, and I had to force it on him. The same with the saddle. I used a double rig with a high-roll cantle, and he snorted at it and kept sidling away and grunted all the time I was tightening the cinches. He stood steady enough when I swung aboard, but when we started off nothing felt right. The saddle was too small for him and sat too high-arched over the backbone and those sloping withers. He kept wanting to drop his head and rub his mouth on his legs over that bit. At last he sort of sighed and eased out and went along without much fuss. He'd decided I was plain stupid on some things, and he'd endure and play along for a while. At the time I thought he was accepting me as boss so I started him really stepping, and the instant he understood I wanted him to move that was what he did. He moved. He went from a walk into a gallop in a single flowing rush, and it was only that high cantle kept me from staying behind. I'm telling you, Mister, that was something, the feel of those big muscles sliding smooth under me and distance dropping away under those hooves.

Then I realized he wasn't even working. I was traveling faster than I ever had on horseback, and he was just loafing along without a sign of straining for speed. That horse just liked moving. I never knew another liked it as much. It could get to him the way liquor can a man and he'd keep reaching for more. That's what he was doing then. I could feel him notching it up the way an engine does when the engineer pushes forward on the throttle, and I began to wonder how he'd be on stopping. I had an idea twelve hundred pounds of power moving like that would be a lot different from eight hundred pounds of bunchy little cow pony. I was right. I pulled in some and he slowed some but not much, and I pulled harder and he tossed his head at the bit, biting, and I yanked in sharp and he stopped. Yes, Mister, he stopped all right.

But he didn't slap down on his haunches and slide to a stop on his rump the way a cow pony does. He took a series of jumps stiff-legged to brake and stopped short and sudden with his legs planted like trees and I went forward, bumping my belly on the horn and over his head and hanging there doubled down over his ears with my legs clamped around his neck.

That Mark horse was surprised as I was, but he took care of me. He kept his head up and stood steady as a rock while I climbed down his neck to the saddle. I was feeling foolish and mad at myself and him and I yanked mean on the reins and swung him hard to head for home and that did it. He'd had enough. He shucked me off his back the way someone might toss a beanbag. Don't ask me how. I'd ridden plenty horses and could make a fair showing even on the tough ones. But that Mark horse wanted me off so he put me off. And then he didn't bolt for the horizon. He stopped about twenty feet away and stood there watching me.

I sat on the ground and looked at him. I'd been stupid, but I was beginning to learn. I remembered the feel of him under me, taking me with him, not trying to get away from me. I remembered how he'd behaved all along, and I studied on all that. There wasn't a trace of meanness in that horse. He didn't mind being handled and ridden. He'd been ready and willing for me to come up and take him in the station corral. But he wasn't going to have a rope slapped at him and be yanked around. He was ready and willing to let me ride him and show me how a real horse could travel. But he wasn't going to do much of it with a punishing bit and a rig he didn't like. He was a big batch of damned good horseflesh, and he knew that and was proud of it and he had a hell of a lot of self-respect. He just plain wouldn't be pushed around and that was that and I had to understand it.

I claim it proud for myself that I did. I went to him and he waited for me as I knew now he would. I swung easy as I could up into the saddle, and he stood steady with his head turned a little so he could watch me. I let the lines stay loose and guided him just by neck-reining, and I walked him back to the ranch. I slid down there and took off the Western saddle and the bridle with that spade bit. I hunted through the barn till I found a light snaffle bit and cleaned it and put it in the bridle. I held it up for him to see, and he took it with no fuss at all. I routed out the biggest of the three English saddles we had for Eastern dudes who wouldn't use anything else and that I'd always thought were damned silly things. I showed it to him and he stood quiet while I slapped it on and buckled the single leather cinch.

"Mark," I said, "I don't know how to sit one of these crazy postage stamps and I'm bunged up some from that beating. Let's take it easy." Mister, that horse knew what I'd said. He gave me the finest ride I ever had. . . .

See what I mean, the best damn horse either of us'll ever see? No, I guess you can't. Not complete. You'd have to live with him day after day and have the endless little things happening tally up in your mind. After a while you'd understand as I did what a combination he was of a serious dependable gent and a mischievous little kid. With a neat sense of timing on those things too. Take him out for serious riding and he'd tend strict to his business, which was covering any kind of ground for you at any kind of speed you wanted. The roughest going made no difference to him. He was built to go at any clip just about anywhere short of straight up a cliff, and you'd get the feeling he'd try that if you really wanted him to.

But let him loaf around with nothing to do, and he'd be curious as a cat on the prowl, poking into every corner he could find and seeing what devilment he could do. Nothing mean, just playful. Maybe a nuisance if you were doing a job where he could get at you and push his big carcass in the way, whiffling at everything or come up quiet behind and blow sudden down your shirt collar. Let him get hold of a bucket and you'd be buying a new one. There'd not be much left of the old one after he'd had his fun. He'd stick his nose in and flip the thing and do that over and over like he was trying for a distance record, then start whamming it around with his hooves, tickled silly at the racket. And when there'd be no one else around to see how crazy you were acting, he'd get you to playing games too. He liked to have you sneak off and hide and whistle low for him, and he'd pad around stretching that long neck into the damndest places looking for you and blow triumphant when he found you. Yes, Mister, that horse liked living and being around him would help you do the same.

And work? That horse was a working fool. No. There was nothing foolish about it. The ranch was still in the beef business too in those days, and he'd never had any experience with cattle before. He was way behind our knowing little cow ponies when it came to handling them and he knew it. So he tried to balance that by using those brains of his overtime and working harder than any of the others. He'd watch them and try to figure what they were doing and how they did it, and then do it himself. He'd try so hard sometimes I'd ache inside, feeling that eagerness quivering under me. Of course, he never could catch up to them on some things. Too big. Too eager. Needed too much room moving around. He couldn't slide into a tight bunch of cattle and cut out the right one, easing it out without disturbing the rest much. And he wasn't much good for roping, even though he did let me use a Western saddle for that soon as he saw the sense to it. Lunged too hard when I'd looped an animal and was ready to throw it.

Maybe he'd have learned the right touch in time, but he didn't get the chance. The foreman saw us damn near break a steer's neck and told us to quit. But on straight herding he couldn't be beat. He could scour the brush for strays like a hound dog on a scent. He could step out and cover territory all day at a pace that'd kill off most horses and come in seeming damn near as fresh as when he started. I used to think I was tough and could take long hours, but that horse could ride me right out of the saddle and act like he thought I was soft for calling a halt.

But I still haven't hit the real thing. That horse was just plain honest all through. No, that's not the exact word. Plenty of horses are that. He was something a bit more. Square. That's it. He was just plain square in everything he did and the way he looked at living. He liked to have things fair and even. He was my horse and he knew it. I claim it proud that for a time anyway he really was my horse and let me know it. But that meant too I was his man and I had my responsibilities. I wasn't a boss giving orders. I was his partner. He wasn't something I owned doing what I made him do. He was my partner doing his job because he wanted to and because he knew that was the way it ought to be with a man and a horse. A horse like him.

Long as I treated him right he'd treat me right. If I'd get mean or stupid with him, I'd be having trouble. I'd be taking another lesson. Like the time along about the second or third week when I was feeling safer on that English saddle and forgot he wasn't a hard-broke cow pony. I wanted a sudden burst of speed for one reason or another, and I hit him with my spurs. I was so used to doing that with the other horses that I couldn't figure at first what had happened. I sat on the ground rubbing the side I'd lit on and stared at him watching me about twenty feet away. Then I had it. I unfastened those spurs and threw them away. I've never used the things again ever, anytime, on any horse. . . .

Well, Mister, there I was mighty proud to have a horse like that but still some stupid because I hadn't tumbled to what you might call his specialty. He had to show me. It was during the fall roundup. We had a bunch of steers in the home corral being culled for market and something spooked them and they started milling wild and pocketed me and Mark in a corner. They were slamming into the fence rails close on each side. I knew we'd have to do some fancy stepping to break through and get around them.

I must have felt nervous on the reins because that Mark horse took charge himself. He swung away from those steers and leaped straight at the near fence and sailed over it. He swung in a short circle and stopped, looking back at those steers jamming into the corner where we'd been, and I sat the saddle catching the breath he'd jolted out of me. I should have known. He was a jumper. He was what people back east called a hunter. Maybe he'd been a timber horse, a steeplechaser. He'd cleared that four-foot fence with just about no takeoff space like a kid skipping at hopscotch.

I'm telling you, Mister, I had me a time the next days jumping him over everything in sight. When I was sure of my seat I made him show me what he really could do, and he played along with me for anything within reason, even stretching that reason considerable. The day I had nerve enough and he took me smack over an empty wagon, I really began to strut. But there was one thing he wouldn't do. He wouldn't keep jumping the same thing over and over the same time out. Didn't see any sense in that. He'd clear whatever it was maybe twice, maybe three times, and if I tried to put him at it again he'd stop cold and swing his head to look at me and I'd shrivel down to size and feel ashamed. . . .

So I had something new in these parts then, a jumping horse bred to it and built for it with a big frame to take the jolts and the power to do it right. I had me a horse could bring me some real money at the rodeos. I wouldn't have to try for prize money. I could put on exhibition stunts. I got together with some of the old show hands, and we worked up an act that pleased the crowds. They'd lead Mark out so the people could see the size of him and he'd plunge around at the end of the shank, rolling his eyes and tossing his head. He'd paw at the sky and lash out behind like he was the worst mean-tempered mankiller ever caught. It was all a joke because he was the safest horse any man ever handled, and anyone who watched close could see those hooves never came near connecting with anything except air.

But he knew what it was all about, and he made it look good. The wranglers would get him over and into the outlaw chute, with him pretending to fight all the way. They'd move around careful outside and reach through the bars to bridle and saddle him like they were scared green of him. I'd climb to the top rails and ease down on the saddle like I was scared too but determined to break my neck trying to ride one hell of a bucking brute. We'd burst out of the chute like a cannon going off and streak straight for the high fence on the opposite side of the arena. All the people who'd not seen it before would come up gasping on their seats, expecting a collision that would shake the whole place. And at the last second that horse Mark would rise up and over the fence in a clean sweet jump and I'd be standing in the stirrups waving my hat and yelling and the crowd would go wild.

After a time most people knew what to expect and the surprise part of that act was gone so we had to drop it. But we worked up another that got the crowds no matter how many times they saw it. I never liked it much, but I blew too hard once how that horse would jump anything and someone suggested this and I was hot and said sure he'd do it, and I was stuck with it. He never liked it much either, but he did it for me. Maybe he knew I was getting expensive habits and needed the money coming in. Well, anyway, we did it and it took a lot of careful practice with a slow old steer before we tried the real thing. I'd be loafing around on Mark in the arena while the bull riding was on. I'd watch and pick a time when one of the bulls had thrown his rider and was hopping around in the clear or making a dash across the open. I'd nudge Mark with my heels, and he'd be off in that forward flowing with full power in it. We'd streak for the bull angling in at the side, and the last sliced second before a head-on smash we'd lift and go over in a clean sweep and swing to come up by the grandstand and take the applause.

Thinking of that since, I've been plenty shamed. I've a notion the reason people kept wanting to see it wasn't just to watch a damned good horse do a damned difficult job. They were always hoping something would happen. Always a chance the bull might swerve and throw us off stride and make it a real smash. Always a chance the horns might toss too high and we'd tangle with them and come down in a messy scramble. But I didn't think about that then or how I was asking more than a man should except in a tight spot that can't be avoided from a horse that's always played square with him. I was thinking of the money and the cheers and the pats on the back. And then it happened. . . .

Not what maybe you're thinking, Mister. Not that at all. That horse never failed in a jump and never would. We'd done our stint on the day, done it neat and clean, gone over a head-tossing bull with space to spare and were just about ready to take the exit gate without bothering to open it. Another bull was in the area, a mean tricky one that'd just thrown his rider after a tussle and was scattering dust real mad. The two tenders on their cagey little cow ponies had cut in to let the rider scramble to

safety and were trying to hustle the bull into the closing-
out pen. They thought they had him going in and were
starting to relax in their saddles when that brute broke
away and tore out into the open again looking for someone on foot to take apart. While the tenders were still
wheeling to go after him he saw something over by the
side fence and headed toward it fast. I saw too, and
sudden I was cold all over.

Some damn fool woman had let a little boy get away
from her, maybe three-four years old, too young to have
sense, and that kid had crawled through the rails and was
twenty-some feet out in the arena. I heard people screaming at him and saw him standing there confused and the
bull moving and the tenders too far away. I slammed my
heels into Mark, and we were moving too in the way
only that horse could move. I had to lunge forward along
his neck, or he'd have been right out from under me.

There wasn't time to head the bull or try to pick up
the kid. There wasn't time for anything fancy at all.
There was only one thing could be done. We swept in
angling straight to the big moving target of that bull,
and I slammed down on the reins with all my strength
so Mark couldn't get his head up to jump and go over,
and in the last split second all I could think of was my
leg maybe getting caught between when they hit and I
dove off Mark sidewise into the dust and he drove on
alone and smashed into that bull just back of the big
sweeping horns.

They picked me up half dazed with an aching head
and assorted bruises and put me on some straw bales in
the stable till a doctor could look me over. They led
Mark into one of the stalls with a big gash from one of

the horns along his side and a swelling shoulder so painful he dragged the leg without trying to step on it. They
put ropes on the bull where he lay quiet with the fight
knocked out of him and prodded him up and led him off.
I never did know just what happened to the kid except
that he was safe enough. I didn't care because when I
pushed up off those bales without waiting for the doctor
and went into the stall that Mark horse wouldn't look
at me. . . .

So that's it, Mister. That's what happened. But I won't
have you getting any wrong notions about it. I won't
have you telling me the way some people do that horse
is through with me because I made him smash into that
bull. Nothing like that at all. He doesn't blame me for
the pulled tendon in his shoulder that'll bother him long
as he lives when the weather's bad. Not that horse. I've
thought the whole business over again and again. I can
remember every last detail of those hurrying seconds in
the arena, things I wasn't even aware of at the time itself.
That horse was flowing forward before I slammed my
heels into him. There wasn't any attempt at lifting that
big head or any gathering of those big muscles under me
for a jump when I was slamming down on the reins. He'd
seen. He knew. He knew what had to be done. That
horse is through with me because at the last second I
went yellow and I let him do it alone. He thinks I didn't
measure up in the partnership. I pulled out and let him
do it alone.

He'll let me ride him even now, but I've quit that
because it isn't the same. Even when he's really moving
and the weather's warm and the shoulder feels good and

he's reaching for distance and notching it up in the straight joy of eating the wind, he's doing that alone too. I'm just something he carries on his back, and he won't look at me. . . .

BLOOD ROYAL
Montgomery M. Atwater

On a famous horse farm in the famous horse-raising State of Kentucky, a colt had his first birthday. His name was Kentucky Roamer, and on this birthday morning he stood restless but obedient at the end of a halter rope, while two men looked critically at him from every angle. The colt looked back at them out of great soft eyes, his ears pricked forward questioningly. Perhaps he sensed that they were not entirely pleased with him.

"Isn't he a beauty?" said one of the men. "Look at that coat and that head."

"Yes, Mr. Harkness," answered the other, "he's all of

that. But what are we going to do with him? He'll never make a racehorse."

"I suppose not; he's too stocky. Where do you suppose he got that build? We haven't had a horse like him that I can remember." Kentucky Roamer's owner looked at him with puzzled eyes.

"He's what a scientific fellow would call a 'reversion to type,'" replied the trainer. "This youngster goes back a couple of hundred years to the true Arab horse. Look at that chest and those shoulders, those solid bones and round feet. That's the real Arab, sir—short and high and square. There's a horse to stick by you and bring you through anything—a wonderful breed!"

Tuckee, as Kentucky Roamer was called, watched the two men attentively. The trainer's long speech meant nothing to him, and he did wish they would let him go.

"You're right," said the owner. "He's the ideal horse, but he just doesn't fit in with us. You'd better train him for my daughter. If he's all you say, he ought to find his place on her ranch."

"I'm glad, sir," said the trainer simply. "He'll be the grandest horse the West has seen since the Spaniards landed in old Mexico."

Four more birthdays passed. Kentucky Roamer was a full-grown horse. Under his gorgeous red skin the long muscles rippled like water, but his mistress seldom took him out for a ride. Tuckee wondered about this and nickered wistfully every time anyone passed. How was he to know that he had grown into too big a horse for a woman and that his mistress was afraid of his high spirit?

One day there was a great rushing about on the ranch:

doors banging, horses and cattle being taken away, trucks driving off with heavy loads. The ranch had been sold. Presently Tuckee himself was put into a big van and driven off to the railroad station.

At the end of a day and a night of rattling and bumping he was led into a strange stall. He smelled dozens of strange horses nearby. Day after day he was taken into a big yard where people he did not know came and stared at him, felt his legs, and looked into his mouth. Sometimes they rode him around the big yard. But always they went away saying regretfully, "Mighty fine horse, but I'd be afraid for my daughter to ride him. Too high strung." Poor Tuckee! He had only pranced a little, just to show how much he would like to go for a real ride!

But one day there came a man who was different from the others. He wore a Stetson hat and a gray-green uniform, with a little bronze badge on which was engraved a pine tree and the words "U.S. Forest Service."

This man did not feel his legs and look into his mouth. He gave the red horse a pat and then just stood and looked, with a light in his eyes that even a horse could read. Kentucky Roamer had found his master!

"A registered Thoroughbred?" said the man at last.

"Yep. I can show you his papers," answered the person in overalls who had taken Tuckee out of his stall. "They don't take much stock in these Kentucky horses out in this country. Can't stand the hardship. We'd make you a nice price just to get him out of the way."

Tuckee noticed that the gray-green man was trembling with excitement as he took a little slip of paper out of his pocket and began to write. . . . As they went out through the gate he nudged his master, by way of making friends, and his master whispered, "You beauty! Maybe you were born in Kentucky, but you're no Kentucky horse; you're an Arab. They must be blind in there."

That day he had his long ride. But before they started his master took him to a blacksmith shop. Tuckee loved that. He stood like a statue and lifted each foot as soon as the blacksmith touched it. His new shoes, instead of being flat, had cleats on the front and back. He stubbed his toes once or twice before he could get used to them. Each time he did it his master laughed at him and said, "Pick 'em up, old fellow! Where we're going, you need those nonskid tires."

They stopped next at a building out of which the gray-green man brought a saddle and bridle. Tuckee could hardly stand still while they were being put on. The saddle was big and broad, not the postage stamp of leather he had been used to. Then, almost before he knew it, the rider was in the saddle. It was good not to have to get down on one knee, as he had been taught to do for his mistress. He pranced sideways.

A touch on the reins turned him down the street, and soon they had left the houses behind. Looming in front of them was a range of tall mountains, green with forest on the sides, white with snow on the peaks. "See those, you old crowbait?" asked the man. "That's where you're going; so slide along, red horse, slide along."

Tuckee lengthened his stride into a running walk that flowed over the ground like water. Up, up into the mountains, where wind sang in the trees and water sang among the rocks. Up into the smell of pine and sage that made a red horse want to run like a startled deer. Kentucky Roamer was going home.

It was early in a June evening when he brought his master to the cabin door. A golden carpet of sunlight still lay on the peaks, although the canyon was in half shadow, when the gray-green man sidled him up to a pasture gate and unlatched it without dismounting. Tuckee had never seen that done before, and he filed his part in the trick away in his memory. Though he had covered a full forty miles since they had left the stable yard, he still walked lightly, easily, as only an Arab can walk at the end of a long day.

But now he smelled other horses and whinnied eagerly, for like all his kind, he loved company. His call was answered. There was the thump of trotting feet, and four horses came toward him out of a thicket of pine trees. The newcomer arched his neck and pranced toward them.

"That's right, make friends," said the gray-green man with a laugh. "You're going to see lots of each other."

One of them, evidently the leader of the band, laid his ears back and snapped at Tuckee's neck. "Here, you," cried the gray-green man, pushing him away with one booted foot, "none of that. I guess, red horse, you'll have to learn to scrap, or old Tony will boss you all over the place."

It was the next day before Tuckee really made the acquaintance of his future companions. After a night in the barn, the gray-green man put him in the corral with the other horses and then sat down on the top rail to watch. Again Tony, the leader, came up with his ears laid back and teeth bared. But this was a game two could play. Instinctively Tuckee flattened his own small ears and struck his tormentor with both front feet. Tony jumped back with an expression of surprise and respect, while the gray-green master laughed and laughed. Once more Tony approached, but this time his ears were pointed forward. Just like a pair of strange dogs, they sniffed noses. Horse fashion, they were shaking hands.

Now that Tony had accepted him, the other horses came up and went through exactly the same performance. Finding that the newcomer was willing and able to stand up for himself, they decided to make friends. In ten minutes they were all standing in a close group, switching flies as if they had known one another for years.

This was the beginning of happy, crowded months for the red horse. He no longer stood for days in a stall, wishing that someone would take him out for a ride. He was a forest ranger's horse, and it was a poor day when he did not carry his master over twenty or thirty miles of steep mountain trails.

Many a time he watched the other horses come in with drooping heads and sweat-streaked sides—something he could not understand, for he had never yet been really tired. He could scramble through the mountains from dawn till dark and reach home tugging at the bit. That was the legacy of his blood—the gift of his Arab forefathers—endurance and courage.

There were dozens of things for Kentucky Roamer to learn in this new life. Most of them he picked up by copying the other horses: to come at his master's whistle or the rattle of the oats can against the barn door, to follow a trail no matter how faint and dim, to remember the way home no matter how tangled had been the course, never to wander more than a few yards when his reins were dropped on the ground. He overcame his instinctive fear of a swamp where he sank to his knees in the mud.

He learned to pick his way through a maze of fallen logs without stumbling, to wriggle among close-set trees without scraping his rider's legs. He could run full speed down a rock-strewn slope without stumbling or breaking his stride. This was life as it should be lived!

Until this year Tuckee had never known much about winter, for he had spent the cold months in his stall, with a blanket to keep him warm. But now the other horses taught him to eat snow when the stream in the pasture froze solid. They taught him how to paw the feathery covering of snow away from the grass when he grew tired of hay. He grew his first long winter coat and soon became more expert in deep snow than any of his companions. Perhaps the reason for this was that he had absolute confidence in his master. If the gray-green man told him by voice and rein that he must plunge through a bottomless drift, he would do so, no matter how terrifying it was to lose his feel of solid ground under his feet.

But winters are long in the mountains, and Kentucky Roamer was heartily tired of this one before spring.

Warm weather came at last, and all the horses were wild with joy. They ran from one end of the pasture to the other, kicking and snorting like colts. Their winter coats began to itch and fall out. They rolled and rolled on the soft spring earth, leaving great patches of hair. Never had Tuckee's coat glistened as it did after he had rubbed away the winter wool. Never had he felt such power in his legs as he did after the green grass came.

And this year he was to need all that strength.

As spring turned to summer he learned a new term: *forest fire*. He heard it so many times each day that it came to have a meaning to him. It meant hot, scorching weather that seemed to suck the energy out of him. It meant a dark pall of smoke hanging over the mountains, filling his nostrils with a pungent, terrifying smell.

Unlike the summer before, there were always a great many people at the cabin of the gray-green man. Trucks came laboring up the canyon at all hours, piled high with boxes and bales, or crammed with men. The pasture was crowded with strange horses, whose milling feet ground the earth to dry powder and whose teeth ripped up every blade of grass. Each day a part of this wilderness army would be swallowed up in the forest, to be replaced before dark. Less often a part of it would return, the men blackened, exhausted, and discouraged, the horses hobbling on sore feet and flinching from saddle sores. Even Tuckee's high spirits felt the drag of anxiety and fear, for he was in the midst of a time of terrible danger to the wilderness: a forest-fire year.

One by one the other horses belonging to the gray-green man gave up under the pressure of desperate work. They grew so thin that each separate rib showed through the skin, and they stood in the barn with hanging heads. At last even Tony could do no more. The gray-green man led him into the barn one night, limping so badly that he could hardly move. Only Kentucky Roamer was left.

Now was the time for the blood of Arab ancestors to prove itself, for Tuckee himself was sick with weariness— Kentucky Roamer, who had never been tired in his life. On the night the ranger tied Tony up for good, the red horse could not eat the dry hay in the manger. Even oats tasted like ashes.

Very early the next morning the gray-green man came into his stall with saddle and bridle.

Tuckee did not arch his neck and prance when the cinch tightened around his body; there was no pleasure now in the thought of another day on the trail. But his head was still high as the ranger led him out of the barn. In the light of dawn he saw drops of water running down the cheeks of his master. "I'm sorry, old fellow," said the man in a crooning voice. "I know you're just about all in. But we're soldiers, and we've got to go. If it would only rain, if it would only rain!"

They rode far that day, thirty miles over the steep mountains. The forest ranger drooped in the saddle, for the man, too, was weary almost beyond his strength.

Suddenly the ranger stiffened; a new forest fire was eating its way savagely through the trees. It was still small, but under the urge of the wind the flames were spreading rapidly. Like one in a dream the gray-green man unstrapped his tools and gave battle. In the path of the fire he began to dig a long trench down through the forest litter to the bare, uninflammable earth. When the flames reached this trench they stopped for lack of fuel, but again and again the wind blew sparks and bits of flaming wood across, so that the fire gained new foothold. The gray-green man was staggering. All that afternoon Tuckee watched while the fire forced his master back and back, gaining headway with each victory.

To the horse it seemed that his master had gone out of his mind. He was gasping, smoke-blackened, wet with perspiration. His efforts had ceased to be systematic. He ran back and forth, lashing at the flames with his ax. The struggle had long ago become hopeless, but he would not retreat.

The forest ranger was chopping frantically at a tree

whose lower branches were afire. In his haste he did not notice another tree, dead and with its roots rotted away, leaning against it. At the second jarring blow of the ax the dead tree shook itself loose and came crashing down upon him, knocking him headlong and coming to rest across his legs. The gray-green man gave a single cry, and then lay still.

Tuckee's first impulse, when the tree fell, was to run away. He started back, snorting with fear. But something stopped him—his reins dangling on the ground. Those trailing bits of leather were a sign that his master wanted him to stay where he was—and he stayed, with the sting of the smoke in his eyes and the fear of fire in his heart.

The flames had put out two long arms on either side of them, and the circle was almost closed when the gray-green man regained consciousness. Tuckee was glad to see him move. Now they would go away from this place. But his master did not get up. He strained at the tree, tried to dig away the earth under his legs with his fingers. But it was no use. Next he pushed himself as high as he could on his arms and looked at the fire. It was coming closer and closer, with fierce snaps and crackles as it consumed the dry underbrush in its path. To the ranger, and to the horse as well, it was bringing a slow and horrible death if they did not escape before those long arms of creeping flame joined hands. "Get up, Tuckee," called the man. "Get out of here!" He seized a small stick and threw it.

The horse did not understand. Was his master trying to tell him to leave? He could not, he would not, until those reins lay against his neck and a man's weight was in the saddle. Again the ranger looked at the fire. Only a few yards away now. After a moment he gave the whistle that always meant, "Come here."

Tuckee did not want to go closer to the creeping monster of flame, but he obeyed. The man looked up at him and said quietly, "It's up to you now, Thoroughbred. If you won't go without me, you'll have to pull me free." As he spoke, he laid hold of the stirrup hanging above his head. Then he ordered sharply, "Now, Tuckee, let's go!"

Kentucky Roamer responded. He felt the drag at the stirrup, and a sickening wrench. He continued to move away from the fire, step by step, sidling so as to avoid stepping on the weight that hung beside him. After several yards he stopped and looked around questioningly.

The forest ranger still clung to the stirrup, his face as gray as dust. As Tuckee stood waiting, the dead tree from whose grasp he had pulled his master burst into flames along its entire length.

The red horse snorted. It was so hot that he felt dizzy. The fire was all around them now, pressing closer. Why did his master delay?

The ranger was stirring, trying to pull himself into the saddle. But both his ankles were broken, and his arms were not equal to the task. He managed to pull himself halfway up, and there he hung, with his useless legs brushing Tuckee's knee.

Kentucky Roamer stood dead still, while his memory went back and back, to a woman who used to scramble at his side in just this way. The picture was dim, but that touch on the leg meant something. He had it now! It meant, "Get down on one knee." At once he dropped down so that his back was only half as high as before.

He heard a gasp of surprise from the man and felt him struggle into the saddle. Like a statue he held his position, as he had been taught, until his rider was firmly seated.

The gray-green man had expended the last of his energy. He simply clung now to the horse's back. But in some way Tuckee knew, as a good horse always knows, that the man was helpless, dependent upon him for his very life. He looked around, seeking a way through the ring of fire. There was only one chance and Tuckee took it. At a quick trot he charged the wall of flame, plunged through it! For a moment it was in his nostrils, burning the hair on his legs, singeing him as high as the mane. But he broke through and plunged away, galloping past the gaunt, smoking trees, kicking up little puffs of ash, fine and gray as dust, at each step.

He must go home, that was the idea firmly fixed in his mind. He must carry his master away from the fire monster to the only place of peace and happiness he knew. But it was a long way for weary, scorched legs to go—all those miles of rocky hillsides and fallen logs.

On and on he struggled. He knew at last the agony of complete exhaustion. The fire monster was far behind. Why not just stop and let that dead weight he balanced so carefully on his back slide off? But the royal blood in his veins, the blood that never surrenders, drove him on.

The world grew dark and a new wind began to blow. Was that night already? Tuckee snuffed the wind without pausing. It was a cool, wet breeze, and the horse knew, though he did not care, that it would rain.

But the cold air was grateful in his parched lungs, and he pushed on a little faster. The ranger seemed to feel it too, for he began to babble and moan. "Rain, Tuckee," he cried. "We've won; we've beaten it!" He sang it over and over in a cracked, harsh voice, "We've won!"

It was midnight when Kentucky Roamer reached that same pasture gate of a year ago. The cold wind still blew, and the gray-green man lay along his neck, a dead weight. Tuckee was sweat soaked and shaking all over. He swung sideways to the gate so that his rider could slip the latch. He had to wait a long time, but at last a shaky hand pushed the latch free, the gate swung open, and Tuckee lurched through.

In front of the cabin he stopped. Voices sounded inside, but it was several minutes before there was a shout, the door opened, and men came running to lift down the gray-green man. They carried him off and Tuckee heard him mumble, "Take care of my horse—saved me."

But no one else heard, and there was no one to watch while his head dropped lower and lower and his legs gradually buckled. With a great sigh he rolled over on his side and his eyelids dropped shut. The first great blobs of rain struck his scorched body with grateful coolness.

Don't think for a moment that Kentucky Roamer was dead. Far from it! All night he lay motionless, with the rain beating down on him. But in the gray morning he got to his feet with a groan and stumbled off toward the barn to find some hay and oats. The rain made him feel hungry, and an Arabian doesn't die so easily as all that.

BREAKNECK HILL
Esther Forbes

Down Holly Street the tide had set in for church. It was a proper, dilatory tide. Every silk hat glistened, every shoe was blacked, the flowers on the women's hats were as fresh as the daffodils against the house fronts. Few met face to face; now and then a faster walker would catch up with acquaintances and join them or, with a flash of raised hat, bow and pass on down the stream.

Then the current met an obstacle. A man, young and graceful and very much preoccupied, walked through the churchgoers and proceeded in the opposite direction. His riding breeches and boots showed in spite of the loose overcoat worn to cover them. He bowed continually, like royalty from a landau, almost as mechanically, and answered the remarks that greeted him.

"Hello, Geth."

"Hello."

"Good morning, Mr. Gething. Not going to church this morning." This from a friend of his mother.

"Good morning. No, not this morning." He met a chum.

"Good riding day, eh?"

"Great."

"Well, Geth, don't break your neck."

"You bet not."

"I'll put a P.S. on the prayer for you," said the wag.

"Thanks a lot." The wag was always late—even to church on Easter morning. So Gething knew the tail of the deluge was reached and past. He had the street almost to himself. It was noticeable that the man had not once called an acquaintance by name or made the first remark. His answers had been as reflex as his walking. Geth was thinking, and in the somber eyes was the dumb look of a pain that would not be told—perhaps he considered it too slight.

He left Holly Street and turned into Holly Park. Here from the grass that bristled so freshly, so ferociously green, the tree trunks rose black and damp. Brown pools of water reflected a blue radiant sky through blossoming branches. Gething subsided on a bench well removed from the children and nursemaids. First he glanced at the corner of Holly Street and the Boulevard, where a man from his father's racing stable would meet him with his horse. His face, his figure, his alert bearing, even his clothes promised a horseman. The way his stirrups had worn his boots would class him as a rider. He rode with his foot "through" as the hunter, steeplechaser, and polo players do—not on the ball of his foot in park fashion.

He pulled off his hat and ran his hand over his close-cropped head. Evidently he was still thinking. Across his face the look of pain ebbed and returned, then he grew impatient. His wristwatch showed him his horse was late, and he was in a hurry to be started, for what must be done had best be done quickly. Done quickly and forgotten, then he could give his attention to the other horses. There was Happiness, an hysterical child, and Goblin, who needed training over water jumps, and Sans Souci, whose lame leg should be cocained to locate the trouble—all of his father's stable of great Thoroughbreds needed something except Cuddy, who waited only for the bullet. Gething's square brown hand went to his breeches pocket, settled on something that was cold as ice, and drew it out—the revolver. The horse he had raced so many times at Piping Rock, Brookline, Saratoga had earned the right to die by this hand that had guided him. Cuddy's high-bred face came vividly before his eyes, and the white star would be the mark. He thrust the revolver back in his pocket hastily, for a child had stopped to look at him, then slowly rose and fell to pacing the gravel walk. A jay screamed overhead, "Jay, jay, jay!"

"You fool," Geth called to him and then muttered to himself. "Fool, fool—oh, Geth—"

From the boulevard a voice called to him. "Mr. Gething —if you please, sir!" It was Willet the trainer.

"All right, Willet." The trainer was mounted, holding a lean greyhound of a horse. Gething pulled down the stirrups. "I meant to tell you to bring Cuddy for me to ride, last time, you know."

"Not that devil. I could never lead him in. Frenchman, here, is well behaved in cities."

Gething swung up. He sat very relaxed upon a horse. There was a lifetime of practice behind that graceful seat and manner with the reins. The horse started a low shuffling gait that would take them rapidly out of the city to the Gething country place and stables.

"You know," Geth broke silence, "Cuddy's got his— going to be shot."

"Not one of us, sir," said Willet, "but will sing Hallelujah! He kicked a hole in Muggins yesterday. None of the boys dare touch him, so he hasn't been groomed proper since your father said he was to go. It's more dangerous wipin' him off than to steeplechase the others."

Geth agreed. "I know it isn't right to keep the brute."

"No, sir. When he was young and winning stakes, it seemed different. I tell you what, we'll all pay a dollar a cake for soap made out 'er old Cuddy."

"There'll be no soap made out of old Cuddy," Gething interrupted him. "I'll ride him out—up to the top of Breakneck Hill and shoot him there. You'd better begin the trench by noon. When it's dug, I'll take him to the top and—"

"But nobody's been on his back since your father said it was useless to try to make him over. Too old for steeplechasing and too much the racer for anything else, and too much the devil to keep for a suvnor."

"Well, I'll ride him once again."

"But, Mr. Geth, he's just been standing in his box or paddock for four weeks now. We've been waiting for you to say when he was to be shot. He's in a sweet temper and d' y'er know, I think, I do—"

"What do you think?"

Willet blushed purple. "I think Cuddy's got something in his head, some plan if he gets out. I think he wants to kill someone before he dies. Yes, sir, *kill* him. And you know if he gets the start of you, there is no stopping the dirty devil."

"Yes, he does tear a bit," Geth admitted. "But I never was on a surer jumper. Lord! How the old horse can lift you!" Gething dropped into a disconsolate silence, interrupted before long by Willet.

"Happiness will get Cuddy's box—she's in a stall. Cuddy was always mean to her—used to go out of his way to kick her—and she, sweet as a kitten."

"So you'll give her his box in revenge?"

"Revenge? Oh, no sir. Just common sense." Any thought of a sentimental revenge was distasteful to the trainer, but he was glad that good Happiness should get his box and disappointed about the soap. It would have lent relish to his somewhat perfunctory washings to say to himself, "Doubtless this here bit of soap is a piece of old Cuddy."

"How long will the trench take?"

"A good bit of time, sir. Cuddy isn't no kitten we're laying by. I'll put them gardeners on the job with your permission—and they know how to shovel. You'll want an old saddle on him?"

"No, no, the one I've raced him in, number twelve, and his old bridle with the chain bit."

"Well, well," said Willet, rubbing his veiny nose.

Willet considered the horse unworthy of any distinction, but in his desire to please Geth took pains to pre-

pare Cuddy for his death and burial. Gething was still
at the big house although it was four o'clock and the men
on Breakneck Hill were busy with their digging. Willet
called them the sextons.

"And we, Joey," he addressed a stableboy, "we're the
undertakers. Handsome corpse, what?" Cuddy stood in the
center of the barn floor fastened to be groomed. He was
handsome, built on the cleanest lines of speed and
strength, lean as an anatomical study, perfect for his type.
The depth of chest made his legs, neck, and head look
fragile. His face was unusually beautiful—the white-
starred face that had been before Geth's eyes as he had
sat in Holly Park. His pricked ears strained to hear, his
eyes to see. The men working over him were beneath his
notice.

"Look at him," complained Joey. "He pays no more
attention to us than as if we weren't here." Cuddy usually
kicked during grooming, but his present indifference was
more insulting. "Huh!" said Willet. "He knows them
sextons went to Breakneck to dig the grave for him. Don't
yer, Devil? Say, Joey, look at him listening like he was
counting the number of spadefuls it takes to make a
horse's grave. He's thinking, old Cuddy is, and scheming
what he'd like to do. I wouldn't ride him from here to
Breakneck, not for a thousand dollars."

He began rapidly with the body brush on Cuddy's
powerful haunch, then burst out, "He thinks he'll be
good, and we'll think he's hit the sawdust trail, or perhaps he wants to look pretty in his coffin. Huh! Give me
that curry. You wash off his face a bit." Cuddy turned
his aristocratic face away from the wet cloth and blew
tremulously.

Joey tapped the blazing star on his forehead. "Right there," he explained to Willet, "but anyhow he's begun to show his age." He pointed at the muzzle that had the run forward look of an old horse and to the pits above the eyes. The grooming was finished, but neither Gething came to the stable from the big house nor the trench diggers from Breakneck to say that their work was done.

"Say, Joey," suggested Willet, "I'll do up his mane in red and yellow worsteds, like he was going to be exhibited. Red and yellow look well on a bay. You get to the paddock and see Frenchman hasn't slipped his blanket while I fetch the worsteds from the office."

Cuddy, left alone, stopped his listening and began pulling at his halter. It held him firm. From the brown dusk of their box stalls two lines of expectant horses' faces watched him. The pretty chestnut, Happiness, already had been transferred to his old box; her white striped face was barely visible. Farther down on the same side, Goblin stood staring stupidly, and beyond were the heads of the three brothers: Sans Pareil, Sans Peur, and the famous Sans Souci, who could clear seven feet of timber (and now was lame). Opposite stood Bohemia, cold blood in her veins as a certain thickness about the throat testified, and little Martini, the flat racer. On either side of him were Hotspur and Meteor, and there were a dozen others as famous. Above each stall was hung the brass plate giving the name and pedigree, and above that up to the roof the hay was piled sweet and dusty smelling.

The barn swallows twittered by an open window in the loft. In front of Cuddy the great double doors were open to the fields and pastures, the gray hills, and the radiant sky. Cuddy reared abruptly striking out with his front legs, crouched, and sprang against his halter again, but it held him fast. Willet, on returning with his worsted, found him as he had left him, motionless as a bronze horse on a black marble clock.

Willet stood on a stool the better to work on the horse's neck. His practised fingers twisted and knotted the mane and worsted, then cut the ends into hard tassels. The horse's withers were reached, and the tassels bobbing rakishly gave a hilarious look to the condemned animal.

Four men, very sweaty, carrying spades entered. "It's done," said the first, nodding, "and it's a big grave. Glad pet horses don't die oftener."

"This ain't a pet," snapped Willet. "He's just that much property and being of no more use is thrown away —just like an old tin can. No more sense in burying one than the other. If I had my way about it, I'd—"

But Geth entered. With his coat off he gave an impression of greater size; like Cuddy his lines were graceful enough to minimize his weight. "Hole dug? Well, let's saddle up and start out." He did not go up to Cuddy to speak to him as he usually would have done, but as if trying to avoid him, he fell to patting Happiness's striped face. She was fretful in her new quarters.

Perhaps, thought Willet, she knows it's old Cuddy's and *he's* gone out for good. All the horses seemed nervous and unhappy. It was as if they knew one of their number was to be taken out to an inglorious death—not the fortune to die on the turf track as a steeplechaser might wish, but ignominiously, on a hilltop, after a soft canter through spring meadows.

Cuddy stood saddled and bridled, and then Willet turned in last appeal to his master's son. "Mr. Geth, I wouldn't ride him—not even if I rode as well as you, which I don't. That horse has grown worse and worse these last months. He wants to kill someone, that's what he wants."

Geth shook his head. "No use, Willet, trying to scare me. I know what I'm doing, eh, Cuddy?" He went to the horse and rubbed the base of his ears. The satin head dropped forward onto the man's chest, a rare response from Cuddy.

Gething led him out of the stable; Willet held his head as the man mounted. As he thrust his foot in the stirrup Cuddy lunged at Willet, his savage yellow teeth crushing into his shoulder. The rider pulled him off, striking him with his heavy hunting whip. The horse squealed, arched himself in the air, and sidled down the driveway. He did not try to run or buck, but seemed intent on twisting himself into curves and figures. The two went past the big house with its gables and numberless chimneys and down to the end of the driveway.

There is a four-foot masonry wall around the Gething country place ("farm" they call it). The horse saw it and began jerking at his bit and dancing, for ever since colthood walls had had but one meaning for him.

"Well, at it, old man," said Gething with a laugh. At a signal Cuddy flew at it, rose into the air with magnificent strength, and landed like thistledown.

"Cuddy," cried the man, "there never was a jumper like you. Breakneck will keep. We'll find some more walls first." He crossed the road and entered a rough pasture. It was a day of such abounding life one could pity the worm the robin pulled. For on such a day everything seemed to have the right to live and be happy. The crows

sauntered across the sky, carefree as hoboes. Underfoot
the meadow turf oozed water, the shad-bush petals fell
like confetti before the rough assault of horse and rider.

Gething liked this day of wind and sunshine. In the
city there had been the smell of oiled streets to show that
spring had come; here was the smell of damp earth,
pollen, and burned brush. Suddenly he realized that
Cuddy, too, was pleased and contented, for he was going
quietly now; occasionally he threw up his head and blew
"Heh, heh!" through his nostrils. Strange that Willet had
thought Cuddy wanted to kill someone; all he really
wanted was a bit of a canter.

A brook was reached. It was wide, marshy, edged with
cowslips. It would take a long jump to clear it. Gething
felt the back gather beneath him, the tense body flung
into the air, the flight through space, then the landing
well upon the firm bank.

"Bravo, Cuddy!" The horse plunged and whipped his
head between his forelegs, trying to get the reins from
the rider's hands. Gething let himself be jerked forward
until his face almost rested on the veiny neck.

"Old tricks, Cuddy. I knew *that* one before you wore
your first shoes." He still had easy control and began to
let him out. There was a succession of walls and fences
and mad racing through fields when the horse plunged in
his gait and frightened birds fluttered from the thicket
and Gething hissed between his teeth as he always did
when he felt a horse going strong beneath him.

Then they came to a hill that rose out of green meadows. It was covered with dingy pine trees except the
top that was bared like a tonsure. A trail ran through the
woods, a trail singularly morose and unattractive. The

pines looked shabby and black in comparison to the sun
on the spring meadows. This was Breakneck Hill. Perhaps
Cuddy felt his rider stiffen in the saddle, for he refused
passionately to take the path. He set his will against
Gething's and fought, bucking and rearing.

When a horse is capable of a six-foot jump into the
air, his great strength and agility make his bucking terrible. The bronco is a child in size and strength compared
to Cuddy's race of superhorse. Twice Geth went loose in
his flat saddle, and once Cuddy almost threw himself.
The chain bit had torn the edges of his mouth and blood
colored his froth. Suddenly he acquiesced and, quiet again,
he took the somber path. Geth thrust his right hand into
his pocket, the revolver was still there. His hand left it
and rested on the bobbing, tasseled mane.

"Old man," he addressed the horse, "I know you don't
know where you're going and I know you don't remember
much, but you must remember Saratoga and how we beat
them all. And Cuddy, you'd understand—if you could—
how it's all over now and why I want to do it for you
myself."

The woods were cleared. It was good to leave their
muffled dampness for the pure sunshine of the crest. On
the very top of the hill, clean-cut against the sky, stood a
great wind-misshaped pine. At the foot of this pine was
a bank of fresh earth and Gething knew that beyond the
bank was the trench. He bent in his saddle and pressed
his forehead against the warm neck. Before his eyes was
the past they had shared together, the sweep of the turf
course, the grandstand aflutter, grooms with blankets,
jockeys and gentlemen in silk, owners' wives with cameras,
then the race that always seemed so short—a rush of

horses, the stretching over the jumps, and the purse or not, it did not matter.

He straightened up with a grim set to his jaw and gathered the loosened reins. Cuddy went into a canter and so approached the earth bank. Suddenly he refused to advance and again the two wills fought, but not so furiously. Cuddy was shaking with fear. The bank was a strange thing, a fearsome thing, and the trench beyond, ghastly. His neck stretched forward. "Heh, heh!" he blew through his nostrils.

"Six steps nearer, Cuddy." Geth struck him lightly with his spurs. The horse paused by the bank and began rocking slightly.

"Sist! Be quiet." They were on the spot Gething wished. The horse gathered himself, started to rear, then sprang into the air, cleared earth mound and trench and bounded down the hill. The tremendous buckjump he had so unexpectedly taken, combined with his frantic descent, gave Gething no chance to get control until the level was reached. Then, with the first pull on the bridle, he realized it was too late.

For a while at least Cuddy was in command. Gething tried all his tricks with the reins, but the horse dashed on like a furious gust of wind. He whirled through the valley, across a ploughed field, over a fence, and into more pastures. Gething, never cooler, fought for the control. The froth blown back against his white shirt was rosy with blood. Cuddy was beyond realizing his bit. Then Gething relaxed a little and let him go. He could guide him to a certain extent. Stop him he could not.

The horse was now running flatly and rapidly. He made no attempt to throw his rider. What jumps were in his

way he took precisely. Unlike the crazed runaway of the
city streets, Cuddy never took better care of himself. It
seemed that he was running for some purpose, and Gething thought of Willet's often repeated remark, "Look at
'im—old Cuddy. He's thinking." Two miles had been
covered, and the gait had become businesslike. Gething,
guiding always to the left, was turning him in a huge
circle. The horse reeked with sweat. Now, thought Gething, he's had enough, but at the first pressure on the bit
Cuddy increased his speed. His breath caught in his throat.
There was another mile and the wonderful run grew
slower. The man felt the great horse trip and recover
himself. He was tired out. Again the fight between master
and horse began. Cuddy resisted weakly, then threw up
his beautiful, white-starred face as if in entreaty.

"Oh, I'm—" muttered Gething and let the reins lie
loose on his neck. "Your own way, Cuddy. Your way is
better than mine. Old friend, I'll not try to stop you
again." For he knew if he tried he could now gain control.
The early dusk of spring had begun to settle on the surface of the fields in a hazy radiance, a marvelous light
that seemed to breathe out from the earth and stream
through the sky. A mile to the east upon a hill was a farm-
house. The orange light from the sunset found every window, blinded them, and left them blank oblongs of orange.
The horse and rider passed closer to this farm. Two collies
rushed forward, then stopped to bark and jump. The
light enveloped them and gave each a golden halo.

Again Gething turned, still keeping toward the left.
A hill began to rise before them and up it the horse sped,
his breath whirring and rattling in his throat, but his

strength still unspent. To the very top he made his way and paused, dazed.

"Oh, Cuddy," cried Gething, "this is Breakneck." For there was the wind-warped pine, the bank of earth, the trench. The horse came to a shivering standstill. The bank looked strange to him. He stood sobbing, his body rocking slightly, rocking gently, then with a sigh, came slowly down onto the turf. Gething was on his feet, his hand on the dripping neck.

"You always were a bad horse and I always loved you," he whispered, "and that was a great ride, and now—"

He rose abruptly and turned away as he realized himself alone in the soft twilight. The horse was dead. Then he returned to the tense body so strangely thin and wet, and removed saddle and bridle. With those hung on his arm he took the somber path through the pines for home.

CHILTIPIQUÍN
William Brandon

A *chiltipiquín* is a little red pepper. There is a poem in Spanish about small women being best, small jewels being best, small horses being best, and small peppers being hottest. A *chiltipiquín* is so hot it is customary to use one *chiltipiquín* to roast another *chiltipiquín,* if you are making cold camp, or so they say. Being small and hot and red together, it gave its name to the colt as a matter of course.

Chiltipiquín, the colt, was foaled in the *manada* of one Luís María Rodriguez, who was not exactly a bandit and cow thief, and not exactly an honest man either, and who dwelled sometimes on one side of the border and some-times on the other, in consequence. It was at the time of

54

an unexpected move across the Rio Grande that his mares were hastily gathered and he found the little red roan among the new yearling colts, but it was not until Don Luís went to stamp the branding iron on his hide that the colt earned his name.

The colt fought the rope and Don Luís and the iron, and he fought the rawhide *peales* brought to tie him quiet, and he fought on until there were four men around him, and until a twitch was finally twisted on his lip to subdue him.

"*Diablo*, but he is a little pet," one of the *vaqueros* said, more or less, calling him Sancho. And another added, "No bigger than a piñon nut. It should seem a man could hold him in his hands."

The others stood by and spoke in uncomplimentary terms of his mother while the colt shivered his stiffened legs at the smell of his burning hair, and then Don Luís stepped back with the iron, wiping the sweat from his eyes.

"He will be called Chiltipiquín," he said, sounding pleased. "He is coal red and fire hot, and he is small. He will be quick. You will be able to tail down a gopher from his back. I like him. He has mixed blood in him. It is my will that he be left a horse. He will be the first possession of my old age," and the old man puffed with pleasure, watching the colt kick and fight the dust when he was released.

They went ahead with their labor in the hot summer sun. It was an odd time for the work and the stock was at an odd age, but these things were sometimes necessary in Don Luís's way of life. That night the Rodriguez household moved to cross the almost dry bed of the river.

Here befell the first calamity. The Chiltipiquín colt, vastly excited by the excitement around him, occasioned by the hopeful yells and occasional shots of the police, the *rurales,* who had suddenly appeared, raced along in the darkness after his mother. She, in turn, was trying, with the rest of the mares, to follow the big red stud who captained the *manada.* They were halfway across the riverbed. The stallion smelled danger and suddenly wheeled, screaming an order to his women and plunging in among them, lashing out with his heels in furious kicks that sounded in great thuds against the mares' barrels, doing his utmost to turn them. Don Luís's *vaqueros* drove into the flank of the melee, and the *rurales* fired twice down into the river flats.

A few of the mares, Chiltipiquín's dam among them, swept on, wild with panic, and thundered into the quicksand the stallion had been trying to avoid.

Chiltipiquín bolted along after them. Don Luís himself saw the red colt flash past him in the moonlight, and, for no sensible reason, he pulled away from his men, trying to work the remaining mares, and built a loop in his rope and dropped it over the head of the colt, who by this time was floundering deep in the bog. Dallying his rope expertly, Don Luís spurred his horse back and pulled the colt free. The mares in the quicksand, struggling frantically, grotesque humping shadows in the darkness, were already down to their shoulders and lost. And Don Luís, standing in his stirrups, saw that the *manada* had broken through the opening he had left and had streamed back to the Mexican side, where the *rurales* waited. It was a bitter loss.

Still, he had his three hundred head of cattle, which

should by now be well across the river. Just as he was thinking that even at around nine dollars for wet stock, they would bring enough to get him up in business again —after a decent interval to let the weather clear—shouts from his men told him that a body of the police had treacherously crossed the river and not only cut off and surrounded his bunch of cows but his *vaqueros* as well. It was against international law, sporting practice, and professional ethics, but it had been done, and Don Luís, enraged, had no choice but to ride fast down the river alone to escape capture himself. He took the Chiltipiquín colt with him.

"I was a *rico*," Don Luís said aloud at his breakfast of half-cooked jackrabbit the next morning, "and now I am reduced to the place of a miserable *charro*. I was a man of good family and fortune, grown old with prosperity and fat with contentment, which enabled me to forget that I was childless and alone. Now I am a nothing." He looked at the colt out of sleepy, red-rimmed eyes and hurled a bone at him. Chiltipiquín jumped away and stopped, facing him again with legs braced.

"Go!" Don Luís said, waving his arms. The colt quivered. "You are the cause of everything! I stopped to save your execrable life, and so I lost my cattle and I lost my men! Go! Out of my sight!" In a fury, Don Luís rose from his fire and ran awkwardly at the colt and threw a stone at him. Chiltipiquín gave a frightened sidewise bound or two and then trotted away, looking over his shoulder. "Go!" Don Luís roared. "Before I waste a bullet on you!"

The colt trotted on and stopped half in the cover of some high chaparral.

Don Luís smoothed his ruffled gray mustaches. "He is a devil," he said. "All red horses are devils. He brought this calamity on me."

Then he sat down again near his dead fire, feeling lonely and out of breath, and his depression grew on him as the sun came up. He was too old for such a defeat. There was nothing for him now but to die. Before Don Luís had lived with the day and lived with the world, and he had devoted his life to the cultivation of a happy philosophy. That at least would always be there to fall back on when everything else was gone. But now it, too, had disappeared, like sunlight blinking out in the evening, and Don Luís was bewildered without it.

Something wet touched the back of his neck, and he yelled and shot to his feet and spun around, and saw the Chiltipiquín colt galloping away to hide in a nearby mesquite thicket. Don Luís yelled curses after him and shook his fists.

"It is not enough," he shouted hoarsely, tears of rage in his eyes, "that you ruin me, but you must come back to kiss my neck! Devil pig dog, go! Go back to your brothers, the *rurales!*" He stuffed the rest of the rabbit in his pocket and kicked the cold fire apart and caught up his hobbled gelding and rode on.

The colt was indeed a devil, stealing up to nuzzle him. What range-bred colt would walk up to a man? Don Luís put his horse at a long Spanish trot while the sun was not yet hot and left the camp of Chiltipiquín far behind. He looked back often to see if the colt was following, but saw nothing of him.

He would feel better now, he told himself. His thoughts would not have been so cold this morning if the colt had not been there to parade like a symbol of what he had lost. He had brought him along last night on his escape without thinking. What did an old man on the dodge want with a yearling colt? It was better to be rid of him. Much better. A little red devil with misfortune bred in his flat bones.

Nevertheless, he did not feel better. When he found shade to lay over for nooning, he was more irritable than before. He thought he would sleep, but found it difficult. He kept starting up, knocking his sombrero off his eyes, thinking he heard things, and finally he crawled up on the rock shoulder at his back to have a look over the country.

He found Chiltipiquín under his nose. The colt had followed him without being seen and, while Don Luís rested, had stood hidden behind the jut of rock. Chiltipiquín saw him at the same moment. His appearance had been weary and disconsolate, but now his head went up and he sidled away a few feet, looking both guilty and wary. There were burrs in his scrubby tail, and the gloss was leaving his coat.

Don Luís, in the act of reaching automatically for another rock, stopped his hand. It was bereavement that showed itself in every line of the colt. His mother had died last night. For that reason the colt had followed him and nuzzled him. With Don Luís was the last vestige of the home smell.

Don Luís sighed and called himself a rough name. "I," he said, "I have lost wealth. You, Sancho Chiltipiquín, have lost more than life itself. I have the stupidity to feel sorry for myself. I am an old burro, Chiltipiquín. My foot is sure, but my brains have gone to ears."

The colt flickered his ears forward at the old man's tone.

"You will stay with me," Don Luís said. "You will be the first possession of my old age."

Chiltipiquín took a hesitant step toward him. Don Luís smiled behind his mustaches and closed his eyes, feeling peaceful in the sun. He opened his eyes again and saw the colt still watching him. He cursed him fondly, and Chiltipiquín stretched his neck curiously and, presently, nickered softly in reply.

From this time on, Don Luís felt better. His soul returned to live once more with him. What, he thought, if the sun did go out in the evening? There was always the afterglow that followed, and to a man of thoughtful philosophy that was the best part of the day.

Through some involved process of reasoning, the old man, now that his first burst of anger and distress was over, thought all the more of the colt because he had saved its life at the expense of all his belongings. He gave some consideration to this and decided it was only human to regard most warmly that which you have helped and to hate most warmly those who have helped you and to whom you are in debt. That the colt did not, therefore, hate him Don Luís filed away as final proof, after all, that horses were not human.

Together they traveled to the rough foothills of the Diablos, where Don Luís's cousin, Estevanico, beat a living from a small outfit. Before reaching Estevanico's *ranchería,* Don Luís killed a prime beef he happened upon and dressed it out and took the quarters to his cousin and his family as a gift. It is never good, Don Luís knew, to visit relatives empty-handed. For Estevanico's daughter, the lovely Rosita, he parted with the valued silver chain from his watch and offered it to her with elaborate casualness as a trinket that might do for a poor bracelet, to jingle on her wrist at the *baile*.

Thus Estevanico and his family were glad to see him, even though they learned later, when they found the hide under a rock, that the steer he had butchered for them had been one of theirs, and Estevanico urged him to stay forever.

"I will stay no more than a lifetime," Don Luís said, chuckling until his cheeks squinted his old, shrewd eyes almost shut, while he took in all the evidence about him of the degree to which Estevanico had prospered since he had last seen him. Beef was going up, and Estevanico, in his slow, plodding fashion, was going up with it. "I am an honest man now," Don Luís said. "That little red colt has made me honest. He is a devil and he does away with all my gains that are too quick, and so I am forced to be honest to live." Here he burst into a roar of laughter, and they all laughed with him.

The months passed smoothly with this august beginning. Don Luís helped Estevanico hunt cows in the fall, and in the winter plaited rawhide, and he broke the roan colt to lead and stand tied.

The next summer Don Luís broke him to ride. It was as he had expected. Chiltipiquín was clever enough to turn on a peg, faster than a ball of fire, willing and full of heart.

So the time passed and Don Luís was content. At Estevanico's he had all the comfort he could want, and in his business he was doing well. He had, early in his stay at his cousin's, formed a quiet working arrangement with

Estevanico's lone hand, a youth named Pedro, and together they drifted out on neighboring ranges frequently and cut out a few head—who would miss them?—and blotched the brands and held them in a hidden corral until occasion offered to run them across the border for a quick sale.

Surely and not so slowly, Don Luís was building up again to his former eminence. The boy Pedro was foolish; he worked for a near nothing; his conscience troubled him, and he seemed to feel that the less he made the less guilty he was. He was, Don Luís learned, hopeful of someday marrying Rosita. It was this dream that had tempted him to listen to Don Luís's arguments and finally to join him in his venture. Don Luís found it touching. As for Pedro's lack of business sense, Don Luís was doing his best to cure him of that before his marriage by letting him do most of the work and get least of the money in their partnership. That was experience for the boy, and was not experience the best teacher? Pedro hoped to make money quickly, so he could be married, for example, and that was admirable, but it illustrated his lack of experience. He would find, after his marriage, that he would need to make money quicker than ever. And, too, Rosita would not stand for such an easy, pleasant way of making money as this, if she knew of it, and Don Luís had an idea Rosita, as a wife, would know of it. She would make a good wife, and good wives always know everything. *Es verdad.*

Amusing himself in this way, giving much thought to what did not concern him, which is the most comfortable kind of thought, Don Luís enjoyed the summer and fall, growing always richer, and he could now take honest pride in his cousin Estevanico's prosperous gather in the beef roundup.

Here befell the second calamity. Don Luís was away when it happened—in town with the wagon, restocking supplies. He returned late in the evening, too late to see the smoke, but he could smell it, and when he swung at a rocking gallop around the cottonwoods to come within sight of the rancho, he saw the outbuildings still smoldering. The main house had not been touched.

They came like the blue norther, Rafael, one of Estevanico's black-thatched younger kids, told him excitedly. They took all the cattle—all—out of the corrals and pens, and they fired the buildings, and they took the *remuda,* and they went away with everything Estevanico owned.

"The colt!" Don Luís cried in a voice of pain. "Chiltipiquín, my red colt!"

They took him, the boy said, beginning to sob. Fighting all the way, but they took him. He had been standing by the house when they had come up, and when one had gone for the house, Rosita had screamed, and the Chiltipiquín colt had kicked the one's horse and broken his leg, and the one had run away from the house, and even now the horse with the broken leg lay dead behind the house.

Don Luís unhooked the near horse of his team and swung aboard him bareback and rode out, while Rafael still talked. He knew what had happened. He had thought, a month ago, that he had been seen at work on a neighbor's stock. And then he had decided that the rider who had come suddenly into view and whirled as suddenly away again had not been near enough to recognize him.

But his horse had been recognized. Chiltipiquín. Everyone knew the red colt. He had been crazy to use him at mavericking. But it was done now.

The neighboring ranchers had done nothing at once. They had known the red colt belonged at Estevanico's, and while they doubtless knew Estevanico well enough to realize that he himself had not been robbing their herds, still they would hold him responsible. Did not the thief, his old cousin, live under his roof?

So they had waited until he had gathered his own stock, and then they had come and taken it away in payment for theirs that Don Luís had stolen. And with it the Chiltipiquín colt.

"They will not take you far," Don Luís said aloud. "I swear it to you, Sancho Chiltipiquín. Not while I live."

He rode on at a lope, following the well-marked trail. He found the colt in a stretch of broken, timbered country near the little hut that was Estevanico's only line camp. Chiltipiquín lay on his side, his flanks heaving, his nostrils dilated, and turned up his head to poke his nose at Don Luís's fumbling hand in the dusk.

The colt's right foreleg was broken. Whether it had happened accidentally or been done deliberately, in payment for the dead horse back at the *rancheria,* did not matter. Don Luís knelt for a long time at the colt's side, his head bowed. When he stood up, finally, Chiltipiquín pawed to rise with him, and Don Luís shouted, "No, stay down!" The colt looked up at him questioningly, and Don Luís rode away quickly. He heard the colt call to him once, a soft begging whinny, and nothing more.

At the *rancheria,* Estevanico was not troublesome, not after Don Luís had given him in cash enough to buy his choused-off stock twice over. Rosita was worse. Pedro, like the fool he was, had confessed to her his part in stealing their neighbors' cattle. But even Rosita was mollified after Don Luís gave her the considerable sum of his wealth he had held out from Pedro for himself and, in a voice of muttering thunder, advised Pedro on living in the future the honest life he was made for. The money, Don Luís said sternly, was a wedding gift.

They were all impressed by the solemnity of his manner. They wondered what he had found out about the colt, but they were afraid to ask him. It was without understanding that they gave him what he wanted, and when Estevanico hesitantly suggested riding with him when he was ready to leave in the wagon, Don Luís refused in a fashion that brooked no further interference.

So he returned to Chiltipiquín with the wagon bed cluttered with equipment and with a lantern for light. He worked through the night making the sling and attaching it to tree limbs overhead and arranging it so it would lift the colt and bear his weight, and when it was ready, he drew the ropes to the wagon, and with the colt's own help brought him up standing, and then drew him yet a little higher, so the colt could not get leverage to kick and harm himself. Now he strapped splints on the broken leg, and here, when Chiltipiquín struggled against the pain, he had a test of the tarp-and-rope sling. It held. When the leg was set, he spent hours again adjusting the sling to the exact position he wanted, where it would allow no possible weight on the colt's off foreleg, but would not squeeze his belly. Chiltipiquín would be living in the sling for a long time.

In the false light of predawn, Don Luís bedded down

between the colt and the wagon and slept. In midmorning he awoke and brought feed from the wagon and water from the stream behind the camp. Then he worked again at the rigging of the sling, and he was engrossed in it when Estevanico spoke soberly behind him. "No horse with a broken leg will ever be right again, never."

"This will." Don Luís gave him an ugly look over his shoulder. "And it will please me if you will stay away. He would be excited."

"I came," Estevanico said, "to tell you we are leaving. We have the money to go someplace else and start better than here. And it would be better for you—"

"I stay with this beast," Don Luís said shortly.

"There is one Villagrá," Estevanico insisted, sounding troubled, "who claims he did not get back a tenth part last night of what he has lost. A friend has told me this morning. It was this one, Villagrá, who tried to take away your Chiltipiquín colt last night. The colt is valuable, he says, and would bring him more money to help make up his loss. I know this one, and he will not give up. He will be looking for you and for the horse."

Don Luís remained silent, working on the sling. The Chiltipiquín colt butted him and knocked off his sombrero and slobbered on his gray hair.

"You cannot live here, old one," Estevanico said. "There is no food."

Don Luís spat. "I will eat grass."

Estevanico went away. He returned later in the day with a load of provisions and Don Luís's belongings, leaving them at the shack, but the old man did not see him. He was asleep again near the colt.

Estevanico looked back, as he left, at the colt, awkward

and comical in the sling. *Ciertamente,* it was a sorrow. One did not save a horse with a broken leg, no matter how fine the horse.

Don Luís thought differently. There was life in his hand, life that would pass into the colt's leg and make it new again.

But the first thing: patience.

"You make me patient, Sancho Chiltipiquín," Don Luís said, "after you have made me honest, for a patient man is honest. What I steal you cause to be taken from me. When I would hurry, you hold me back. You are one possession for my old age, in truth."

He came on tracks once, sign of a ridden horse, at the edge of the woods, almost within sight of the line camp, and for a few days he woke up at odd hours and walked out quietly to listen, but he saw no one. The time passed and he forgot to worry. He worked too much with the Chiltipiquín colt to have time left for worry.

There came the day that the sling was gently moved again, and the colt stood square on all four legs. Square— Don Luís walked around him time and again, his heart in his throat—square as a box. He was anxious, the red colt, to try his leg now. He was restless and thin. He bit at the sling and stomped his feet, the off forefoot gingerly at first and then with abandon, pleased at the way it worked.

But it took time. At first he walked, led, until the last trace of shortness was gone from the leg, and then cautiously trotted, still to the rope, with Don Luís running beside him, blowing and fat and clumsy.

Winter came near and a snow sprinkled the trees and melted in an hour. Chiltipiquín ran, with Don Luís on his

back. He pivoted and turned; he skidded to a stop when
Don Luís dabbed a loop on a stump. He ran figure eights
among the trees and threw up clods of dirt to explode
among their branches. The leg was well.

"So," Don Luís said, chuckling, "who wins, my Chiltipiquín? So how do you keep me honest, when you can
now outrun the *rurales?*"

The colt raised his head and snorted.

"We will see," Don Luís said. "We are both hungry.
We will see. You have given me a lesson in patience.
Soon now we will go on with our life, and we will see."

Here befell the third calamity. Don Luís's food was
low, and he went out on foot after a bird or a rabbit. He
had set snares, and he inspected these, and it took a good
while. When he returned, the colt was gone. As before,
there was sign of a struggle, but it had ended with Chiltipiquín leading quietly away. Probably they had blind-
folded him.

In his madness, Don Luís did not trail them. He was
afoot; they would outdistance him anyway. Instead, he
walked the eleven miles to the Villagrá spread. He
reached it after dark and found it deserted.

The next day he appeared in town, haggard and exhausted. He sold his silver-mounted saddle and bridle
and his guns, and he rode out in a wagon with the pur-
chaser to the line camp to get them. He could have
knocked the man in the head and left with the wagon
team. Instead he took his money and went back to town.
After another twenty-four hours he had learned what he
wanted to know.

"Patience," he said to himself, "patience, old man. Patience, old one," and he looked at his trembling hands

and cursed them softly, his eyes smiling in their pouches of fat. He was old.

He hired to work with a freighter hauling north, going up empty for another load of goods. It would be a fast trip.

Winter had settled down in Kansas, but at the sale barn there were still auctions every Saturday, and they would continue as long as the late trail stuff was consigned to them.

The owner of the barn liked the stallion so well that he had thoughts of keeping him for himself. Maybe he would bid him in if his price didn't get high enough. Strange that a trail bunch would be carrying this stud with them. Mexican outfit, man named Villagrá. Horse might be stolen. Road brand on his left shoulder, an old curlicued Mexican monogram brand under it. Well, somebody came up with a horse to trade for beef. Throw him in with the cavy, the trail boss said, and then it turns out he's a stud. And what a stud.

Hot, though. Vicious-tempered brute. No one in the barn could handle him except that old Mexican he'd hired a couple of days ago. Damn fool horse treated him like an old friend.

Mexican horse, through and through, that was it. You'd have to talk to him in cowpen Spanish.

"Hey, there, you *viejo!* Get away from that red son of a dog for a minute and muck out this floor! There's a sale tomorrow."

"*Sí señor,*" Don Luís muttered hastily.

Chiltipiquín poked his nose and nudged him as he scrambled away and knocked off his ragged hat.

"It is the last thing I will steal," Don Luís said, chuckling. "I swear it to you."

It was almost morning. The sale barn was eighty miles behind them. The snow was not deep and the day would be clear. Soon the snow would be less, and then it would be gone, and the southern country would come over the horizon to meet them.

"Three misfortunes, Sancho Chiltipiquín," Don Luís said. He shivered in his threadbare clothes and felt his age in his bones, but his voice smiled. "Three misfortunes make a life. That is an antique proverb. Now we walk with God."

"Walk with God," Chiltipiquín said.

Perhaps the old man only imagined the words in the hiss of the morning wind over the snow and the rattle of bit rings as the colt tossed his head, or perhaps the red colt said them. Perhaps.

Quién sabe?

THROW YOUR HEART OVER
Stuart Cloete

Helen heard her father say, "She's—she's not going to die, is she?" *She* was the she, her. It's me they're talking about, she thought.

"No, John," Smitty said. Doctor Smith was his real name, but nobody called him that. "There's even a bit of improvement."

"How long will it take her?" Daddy said.

"I don't know, Johnnie. You see, we don't even know just what she's got. It's not polio—at least not an ordinary polio. It's something different—something new. If only this were America instead of South Africa. They know more there. In ten years—"

"Ten years," her dad said. "In ten years she'll be twenty-one and I'll be forty-two. . . . Marriage, children. What's there for her? What'll her life be?"

"She's not going to die, Johnnie. There's some improvement. Let's leave the rest to God. There is a God, you know. That's something we doctors find out."

"Expecting a miracle, Smitty?" her dad said.

"There are miracles too. Wonderful things still happen. Things that cannot be explained."

"Like her being struck down with this thing—an innocent child."

That's me, Helen thought. I'm an innocent child. The idea pleased her. Then she thought about God. She thought He must be something like her grandfather. Bigger, of course, with a bigger white beard, but resembling him in many ways. It was interesting to lie here and hear every word they said in the adjoining bedroom. Of course, they didn't know about it. How could they, since she didn't talk to herself?

Then Smitty said, "The kid's bored. She's an outdoor girl. What about a pony? Ever think of a pony, Johnnie?"

Helen pulled herself up in bed and clasped her hands together.

"A pony?" her father said. "You think she could ride?"

"One of the boys could hold her on. Old Herman, for instance. She could get around and see the veld again. The thorns are in bloom now. Yellow," the doctor said. "Yellow and perfumed." In her mind Helen saw the little fluffy yellow balls of the thorn flowers and smelled them. "I'm going to ask her," Smitty said.

"I can't buy a pony," her father said. "I can't even pay you."

The door banged and Smitty was in the room. "Do you want a pony, Helen?" he said.

"No, I don't want a pony, Doc."

"It would do you good. You could get out. Get around again. Old Herman could hold you on."

Helen gripped the sides of her bed again and leaned forward. The round white enameled bars were hard and cold in her hand. Something big was happening. She was on the edge of an event. Like a precipice, a vast space loomed ahead and below her. This was her opportunity. She had always wanted a pony. But not now.

"Ponies are for kids, Doc," she said. "I want a horse, a real horse. I'm a girl now. I'm not a kid anymore."

In her mind she saw the horse—a milk-white Arab with a flowing mane and tail. She stared into his liquid eyes. She felt his hot breath in her face. Tears came into her eyes. She brushed her hair back from her face and stared at Smitty and her dad. They looked very big standing there looking down at her in her bed.

"All right, a horse. Do you want one? Do you want to get out?"

Smitty was close to her now. She could smell him. She smelled tobacco, whisky, tweed, dog, and the hair stuff he used. His eyes, behind the thick lenses of his glasses, were enormous. She stared into them. She drowned herself in them. I'll marry him, she thought. If he'll wait till I'm grown up and well, I'll marry him. The tears ran down her cheeks. They were salt in her mouth. She could not speak. There was so much she wanted to say, and all she could do was to cry like a baby, like a kid.

Smitty had her wrist in his hand. She could feel his strength pouring into her. She pulled herself together.

"Yes," she said, "oh, yes. A horse. I want to get out."
In her mind she saw it all again: the veld, the thorns, the
rocks, the cattle, the tall golden grass bent before the
wind, the weaver birds' nests hanging like grass balls
from the swaying branches of the willows by the spring.
She was sobbing now and he held her. Smitty was holding
her. Everything was going to come right. There were
Smitty and God and a horse.

Then her mother came in. She held her, too, and her
father patted her hand. I'm too small, she thought. If I
was bigger, everyone could hold me. She wanted everyone
to hold her.

She knew why her mother hadn't been with them.
Helen knew she had been afraid of what Smitty might
say after he had examined her. Her mother was beautiful. Fair skin with big blue-gray eyes. She smelled of
lavender. Dad smelled of gas and grease and oil. Once
he had smelled of a farm—of cows and milk and manure
and hay all mixed up with tobacco and sweat. He worked
for Mr. de Wet of the Central Garage now, and Mother
ran the farm. It was the only way they could make ends
meet, they said, since the drought had hit them. Three
years of drought and only one spring—the one where
the willows with the weaver nests were still strung. Helen
often wondered what meeting ends were. What happened
when ends did meet? When they didn't, the cattle died
and Dad went to work for Mr. de Wet. Before that he'd
been on the farm. But she had been too small to notice
what went on. I was just small and happy then, she
thought. Just a baby.

Vaguely, half asleep, she saw Smitty open the door for
her mother and pat her shoulder. "You're a good girl,

Grace," he said. It was funny to hear him calling Mother a girl. But Daddy did, too, sometimes. Grown-ups were really very funny. There was no way of understanding them—except Smitty. There was something about him with his big owl eyes. Of course, it was the glasses that made them look so big. But I'd like to marry him, she thought. The horse, the milk-white horse, was all due to him. The dream that was going to come true. When she'd been well she hadn't wanted a horse or pony. Why should she, when she could run about so fast on her own two legs? But since she had been ill she'd thought about horses a lot. Looked at pictures of horses galloping. How wonderful that must be, to be on the back of a galloping horse.

The last things she remembered were her dad standing at the door looking back at her and the click of her mother's heels on the staircase. Smitty must be waiting for Dad.

In the old car on his way back to the garage Johnnie Blackett went over what Smitty had said. No worse . . . getting better . . . trust in God . . . a horse. . . . A horse. What was the old story? For lack of a nail a shoe was lost, for lack of a shoe a horse was lost, for lack of a horse a battle was lost. . . . "A horse, a horse, my kingdom for a horse." That was Shakespeare, or at least he thought it was. For lack of a horse my daughter may be lost.

He'd never forget the look in her eyes, big as saucers— she had Grace's eyes—with tears balanced like drops of dew in the corners, and her remark, "Ponies are for kids. I'm a girl now." A girl, and in just a few years she'd be ripe for life, for love. Horses seemed to mean a lot to her. She had never mentioned it before. Perhaps because she was ill. Perhaps because as long as it wasn't mentioned it could not be refused. She was an old-fashioned kid with plenty of courage and a mind and will of her own. That frail little fairylike creature made of ivory and gold had a will of steel. And Smitty had seen it and thought of an answer. If she set her mind on anything, she'd do it or die in the attempt.

He remembered what his father had told him when he began to jump his first pony, "Throw your heart over first, Johnnie, and you'll follow it, Johnnie boy." After that he'd never been afraid. She was like that. But a horse. . . . Horses cost money. There weren't even any horses around to look at and maybe borrow anymore. Ten years ago a dozen men would have lent him a horse. Ten years ago he could have bought a dozen horses.

He looked out at the veld as he drove along the red dirt road. How beautiful it was. Rolling country dotted with clumps of bush and isolated thorns, all splashed with the gold of spring. Soon it would be summer, and they might get good rains this year.

When Johnnie got to the garage he was surprised to find it unchanged. It looked exactly as it had looked yesterday. But yesterday was so long ago. So much had happened since then. How afraid he had been when he drove home to talk to Smitty. Helen was going to live. She was better. She might get well. If only I could get her a horse, he thought. Such a simple thing, really—or it used to be. By now even in Africa a horse was a rare animal, apart from valuable show horses and so on. The ordinary farm riding horses had all disappeared.

Hendrik de Wet came out of the front office to greet him. "Everything O.K., Johnnie?" he said. He meant about Helen, of course. By this time everyone in Boom-spruit would know that Smitty had made a new and detailed examination after the specimens came back from the laboratory in Johannesburg.

"O.K. At least she's no worse, and he holds out hope. Slow, of course. But hope."

"Slow but sure," de Wet said. "That's the ticket." He was an Afrikaner and given to such phrases. He became businesslike. "The tractors have come, Johnnie. They're on the siding. Get them down and line 'em up—like soldiers," he said. "Like a lot of bloody *rooisbadgies* (redcoats)." He laughed, a big booming laugh that shook the belly that hung out in a great shaking ellipse below his belt.

"Nice and straight," he said. "All six of them so that the farmers can't miss them. Spring," he said. "The plowing season. We'll borrow some plows from the store—three furrow plows and disks—and hook them up. Give 'em the idea." He became confidential and took Johnnie's arm. "Farmers," he said. "Got to show 'em. You've got to put two and two together for 'em. See the tractors, and they'll never think of plows. See the plows, and they'll never think of tractors." He seemed to have forgotten that Johnnie was a farmer.

Two hours later the bright red tractors were aligned with not a six-inch difference between them and each had a plow or a disk hooked on behind it. "All done," he said to de Wet. "Come, Kyk. Look at 'em. Pretty as a picture."

They stood together in the sunlight looking at the

scarlet tractors glistening in their clean uniforms of paint.

"Pretty," de Wet said. "Beautiful!" He stroked the hood of the one nearest to him.

"See the horses, Johnnie?" he said.

"What horses?"

"In the sale yard. Stock sale tomorrow, you know. Wednesday. The old and the new," de Wet said. "Tractors coming in, and the farm horses going out. This lot must be about the last around here. That's why I got the tractors down. I heard a lot of farmers were selling horses to a dealer and jumped in. Took a risk, of course. But a calculated risk. That's business, Johnnie boy. That's what I like."

"Mind if I go up and look at them?" Johnnie said.

"Look at what?"

"The horses."

"No. Sure, go ahead. If you see any of the sellers, bring 'em back to see these beauties." He spoke as if the tractors were chorus girls. "No deposit. Easy terms. Go ahead, my boy." He patted him on the back. Hendrik de Wet was a great patter. Men on the shoulder, children on the head, and women—well, he patted them, too, wherever he could.

The horses, all oldish farm animals, most of them much the worse for wear, work, and a long truck ride, stood with lowered heads in the stock kraal. Grays, blacks, bays; there wasn't much to choose among them.

As Johnnie went up and leaned his arms on the rails, one horse, a roan mare that he had not seen before, looked up and came toward him. When she was about a yard away she stopped and extended her nose toward his hands. Her nostrils were wide open. She blew through them softly. Her eyes, one of them a walleye, looked into his. A horse, my kingdom for a horse. . . . For want of a horse my daughter was lost. "Remember there's still a God," Smitty had said.

While he and the roan were looking at each other a tall, thin, sunburned man came up to him. "Dog meat," he said. "That's what they are. More's the pity. And to think I've come down to this. There's no good or bad horses no more. Just fat and thin. That's all, Mister. Imagine judging men that way, for their worth—fat or thin."

"Yours?" Johnnie said.

"Mine. I was a horse dealer once—real horses, I mean. Saddle horses, cart horses, mares for breeding, studs, even a blood horse now and again. Do you think I like it?" He turned on Johnnie savagely. "Man," he said, "I love horses. Take her, for instance"—he jerked his head at the mare—"that's a good 'un. A good mare. I've never seen a bad roan yet. And I like a walleye. No, she's not blind in it." He caught her head collar—she was close to them now—and flashed his hand over her blue eyes. "See her wink," he said.

God, Johnnie thought, God sent Smitty. God sent the roan. God sent the dealer. God told Hendrik to tell me. "Will you sell her?"

"Sell? Of course, I'll sell her, and much sooner to you than to the knacker."

"How much?"

"Do you know how they sell horses today, Mister?"

"How do they?"

"By the pound. Like butter or cheese or old iron. A bad horse is worth as much as a sound one. Meat, that's

what they are. Not horses anymore. Just dog meat. Meat
for pets." He spat in the dust with disgust. "Old horses,
yes, old worn-out horses. That's one thing. But her—she's
not even aged. Nine years old she is. With nine years of
work left in her and nine good foals if you want to breed
her. She's bred before. Roomy," he said. "If you put her
to a blood horse, you'd get something. But nobody'll wait
no more. Nearly a year's gestation. Three more years for
the foal to come to hand. But what's four years when you
think of the pleasure of it?"

"How much?" Johnnie asked again.

"Thirty pounds, Mister, and that's what she cost me,
more or less, but I'll make enough on the others."

"Will you hold her for me while I get the money?"
Hendrik would advance it to him. "Will you wait?"

"I'll wait. I got to hang around anyway till the sale
tomorrow. You'll find me at the hotel. Ask for Frank
Sparrow. Sparrow, the horse dealer."

As Johnnie turned to go, Sparrow said, "Listen, Mister,
this is a deal you can't lose on. You take her. You'll feed
her up a bit naturally, and if you don't like her I'll buy
her back any day and give you a profit. Can't lose, man,"
he said to Johnnie's back, "and there's not many deals
like that in the world today."

Hendrik de Wet began to laugh when Johnnie told him
what he wanted the thirty pounds for. "Man," he said,
"this is 1959. What do you want a horse for?"

"She's a good mare," Johnnie said, "a roan with a
walleye on the near side, and only nine years old—too
good for dog meat."

"Man, you're so bust you've got to borrow to buy her. What is it? You going soft or something?"

"I'm not soft, de Wet," Johnnie said. "No, I'm hard as hell. So hard that I'll chance everything on this gamble."

"You're not going to race her?"

"I am, Hendrik."

"When? How?"

"I'm going to race her with death, and the stakes are high."

"You're mad, Johnnie."

"I'm not. It's Smitty."

"The doctor?"

"Yes. He thinks if I can get Helen on a horse, she has a chance."

De Wet pulled out his pocketbook and counted out six fivers. "Here you are, Johnnie, and it's not a loan. You've done more than your job here."

"I'll pay you back, Hendrik."

"In your own time when you're on your feet again." Johnnie took his hand. They turned away from each other, embarrassed by their unaccustomed emotion. Each had seen something in the other that he had not known existed, for neither had thought the other had a heart.

Mr. Sparrow was in the bar of the Jacaranda Hotel fondling the ears of a crossbred ridgeback with one hand and holding a glass of beer in the other.

Johnnie sat down beside him and put the money on the table. "Here's the thirty quid."

Sparrow put down the glass and stuffed the money into the breast pocket of his coat. "I'm glad," he said.

"She was too good for it. It's not her time yet. You know, Mr.—"

"John Blackett," Johnnie said.

"Mr. Blackett," Sparrow went on, "we all come to it— man and horse and dog. One day we'll all come to the end of our tether. But it should be the end, not in the middle, like"—he paused—"nor the beginning."

"Beginning?'

"I lost a boy in the Second World War," he said. "Nineteen he was. And he had the making of a good 'un, though I says it myself."

"That's why," Johnnie said.

"Why what, Mr. Blackett?"

"I want her."

"Go on, tell me."

"It's for my girl. She's paralyzed, and the doctor thinks riding might help her. I only wonder if she can hang on. It's her legs, you know."

Mr. Sparrow put a brown veiny hand on his knee. "She's alive, Mr. Blackett. That's something. That's a lot."

Johnnie got up. They shook hands. He seemed to be shaking hands with everybody today. "I'm going to say something," Johnnie said, "and if you laugh I'll knock you down." His eyes blazed. "I think God sent you, and I don't believe in God. At least I didn't."

Then he turned and went out of the bar. The big ridgeback wagged its tail slowly from side to side and looked up at Mr. Sparrow.

Now it was a matter of getting the mare home. It was only five miles, and Johnnie arranged with Franz, the boy who did odd jobs around the garage, to take her.

"I'll tell you when," he said, "and take you up to get her."

"*Ja, baas.*" Five bob he was getting. That was a whole day's wage, and the *baas* was driving him back in his car. It was like Christmas. Man, if this happened every day, what a life he would lead!

At five o'clock Johnnie took Franz up to the kraal and they caught the mare. It was not difficult. She seemed to recognize him when he called her and came up to him on her own.

She led easily. It would take Franz only an hour or so to get her back to the farm. Johnnie drove fast and went straight to Helen's room, and with her wrapped in a blanket on his knees he waited on the stoep with his eyes fixed on the farm road till he saw them coming. The black man walked easily, tirelessly. Five miles was nothing to him. The mare followed like a dog, the riem he was holding hanging slack in a loop.

Helen saw them almost as soon as he did. "There's a boy coming, with a horse, Daddy," she cried. "A boy with a horse, and they're coming this way. We'll see them. Oh, Daddy, we'll see them." To see anything had become an event for Helen.

The man and the horse got bigger.

"It's Franz," Helen said, "with a roan."

"Certainly looks like it," Johnnie said.

"It's late," Helen said. "Perhaps they could stay the night. Perhaps you could put me up on the horse for a minute, Daddy, and we could play pretend."

"Pretend what, darling?"

How stupid could grown-ups be? "That he's ours," she said, "our very own horse."

"We'll see, darling."

Franz pulled up at the stoep. He tied the riem to the rails. "Here you are, *baas*."

"What's he mean, Daddy?"

"What he says."

"He said 'Here you are.' " Helen was wriggling like an eel in her father's arms.

"Well, here she is, Helen," Johnnie said. "Your horse."

"Oh . . . oh, she's really ours!"

"She's yours, darling. With compliments of Dr. Smith and Mr. Hendrik de Wet."

"Put me up, Daddy. Put me up."

"She's filthy."

"Never mind. Mother can wash me again. Oh, please, please." She clasped her hands together as if she were praying.

Her mother came onto the stoep. "What is it, Johnnie?" she said.

"I bought a mare, Grace, and Helen wants me to put her on her back, but she's too dirty."

"Put her up, Johnnie. The child will wash and so will her pajamas."

"Put me up, Daddy. Mother says I can. Mother says—"

Johnnie lifted her onto the mare's back and held her there. The horse turned her head and nuzzled the child's knee.

"Oh," Helen said, "she's got blue eyes. Just like Mother."

"Only one eye," Johnnie said.

"One of each," Helen said. "One like Mother's and one like yours. How wonderful!"

Johnnie laughed. It was grand to see her so happy. Then he took her down. "Bed now," he said, "and another bath. Tomorrow we'll wash her. I've got to drive Franz back to the dorp now." He kissed his daughter and put her into her mother's arms.

Helen spent all the next day in the kraal sitting on a box beside the mare, listening to her munching hay and crunching mealies. Old Herman sat watching them both, smoking his pipe.

Everything the mare did was wonderful. The way she ate. The way she drank from the bucket Herman brought her. The way she rolled, kicking her legs in the air. When she'd done all this, the horse came and stood beside the girl with her soft gray nose almost in her lap, while Helen stroked her face and pulled her ears.

Her father found them like that. He had come home early to wash the horse. It took five washings with soap and water to get her clean enough to satisfy Helen. Then she was dried with a whisk of hay and rubbed down with a bit of sacking. Her tail, mane, and forelock were combed with a metal comb Johnnie had picked up in the dorp, and the long hairs on her heels were trimmed off with Grace's dressmaking scissors. She looked a very different animal now.

"She's lovely," Helen said, "ever so lovely."

"Wait till tomorrow. When she's really dry we'll brush her." Johnnie threw an old blanket over the horse and fastened it in place with a surcingle. "Bedtime, Helen," he said. "Bedtime for you both."

Old Herman led the mare off to a shed that had been

bedded down with veld grass, and Johnnie carried his daughter into the house.

Before he went to work Johnnie went to look at the mare. She raised her head and neighed when she saw him. He went up to her, and she rubbed her head against his chest. He gave her some crusts of bread he had brought from breakfast.

This was not the same horse, not the same horse at all. He wished Mr. Sparrow could see her now.

Life on the farm now changed its pattern. Where Helen had been the center, the axle around which the wheel of their lives revolved, it was now the mare, because it was around the mare—which Helen had named, for some reason, Old Lucy—that Helen herself revolved. Old Lucy and old Herman, who took care of both her and Helen.

There was a regular routine. In the morning Lucy was saddled. The saddle consisted of a pillow fastened with a surcingle. Lucy also wore a head collar with a riem that Herman held with one hand while he balanced Helen with the other. In this fashion they covered the whole farm and even went beyond it. In the afternoon Helen rested, and Old Lucy grazed near the homestead. In the evening Helen rode again.

Every day the mare put on condition. Every day she became more tame, more human. "More like a dog than a horse," Grace said.

"Perhaps more horses would be like dogs if they were treated like dogs," Johnnie said.

Helen didn't need Herman to hold her on anymore now. She managed very well with her fingers twisted around the mare's mane. Sometimes she even managed a slow canter with Herman running in front of the horse. But they were always out of sight of the house when she tried something new. She was getting better—stronger—she could feel it.

I'm going to surprise them all one day, she thought. And happy. She'd never been so happy before. But perhaps you had to be unhappy before you could be happy.

Sometimes the Metz children came over to play with her and ride Old Lucy. Charmian was twelve, a year older than Helen, and Charlie was ten. They were nice children. They always brought an apple or sugar for Old Lucy. Their daddy brought them over in the afternoon, and Helen's daddy drove them home when he got back from work. Helen always sat on the front seat beside him.

One day after they had been coming for about a month, Charmian said, "Can we try to jump her, Helen?"

It seemed a great idea and the children rolled out two empty five-gallon dip drums, leaving them on their sides, and set a blue-gum lath across them. Charlie led Lucy up to the jump and told her about it.

"Jump it, Charm," he said to his sister. "You show her how."

Charmian jumped. Then she said "Let's see if she'll follow." She led Lucy back a few yards and ran to the jump with the mare cantering behind her. She never hesitated, and the two came over side by side.

Helen clapped her hands. "Again," she said, "do it again!"

"Give her an apple," Charlie said.

They gave Lucy half an apple and went over the jump again. "She likes it," Charmian said. "I'm going to try riding her over." She climbed onto Lucy's back with

Charlie's help. The horse seemed to like this even better.

"I'll stand them up," Charlie said. "What about that?"

"O.K.," his sister said. "We'll try it." She patted the horse's neck. The boy stood the drums up on end.

Lucy cocked her ears and popped over.

Helen, sitting on the grass with Herman behind her, was entranced. It was wonderful. It was beautiful the way Old Lucy came up to the jumps and took them clean. Like a buck, flying like a bird through the air. Her coat of alternate chestnut and white hairs shone like shot satin. Her mane and long tail flowed. Her forelock divided itself into two plaits, one each side of the white star on her forehead. Beautiful, that's what it was, with the blue, cloudless sky above and the chickens scratching in the veld behind the sheds and kraals where they had set up the jumps.

After this they jumped almost every day with an audience of Grace and old Herman, Mr. Metz and Johnnie in the evening. Mrs. Metz came over, too, sometimes, to watch. The jumps were regular jumps now—three feet high—the gum laths resting on pegs set into poles Herman had sunk into the ground.

After this there was no doubt about Helen's improvement, Smitty said. It was not so much her legs. There was very little difference there. But in her general health, the brightness of her eyes, in her happiness. She was, as he had said before Old Lucy came, an outdoor girl who was pining away in the white cage of her bedroom.

That was how the conversation started. Then it came out. "I've arranged for her to go into a hospital for some tests in Johannesburg," Smitty said. "There's a man there now, an American specialist, who's interested in her case."

"Soon?" Johnnie said. "How long is he going to stay?"

"Now," Smitty said. "He's got to get back, so I'll drive her in tomorrow."

"How much will it cost?" Grace asked.

"Not too much. They're friends of mine at the nursing home."

"We'll manage," Johnnie said.

Grace turned to her husband. "I'll go with her and stay with Muriel. You can manage for a bit, can't you, Johnnie?"

"I'll manage." He knew he could manage, and the farm did not need much attention now. They couldn't plow till it rained, and the few cattle they had left could take care of themselves. All they needed was a dipping once a week and he'd do that on Sunday.

Lucy was the only thing that worried Helen. This was adventure. It was change. She had never been in a big town. She said, "Lucy? She'll miss me. You'll look after her, Daddy?" Her voice was anxious.

"I'll look after her, darling."

"Talk to her, Daddy. She likes to be talked to, especially while she's eating."

What a wonderful kid she was. No thoughts about herself at all. Just her horse. But the horse had become almost a part of her—a symbol of activity.

"I'll talk to her," he said, "and the Metz kids will be over every day, I expect."

"Bed now," Grace said, and that was the way the

evening ended, with Smitty smoking his pipe in silence and Johnnie thinking how lonely he would be.

And Johnnie was lonely. There were letters from Grace almost every day, but there was no Grace to come home to, and he picked the letters up at the post office in the dorp. No little girl to be carried in his arms. No talk of Old Lucy and how wonderful she was.

It was to have been a month, but it was longer and the bills were coming in. Not big bills, Smitty had been right. They were cutting things to the bone, but they were bills and they had to be met.

The cattle went. The two last boys were paid off. Only old Herman stayed on.

Johnnie was standing by the spring looking at the weaver birds' nests, just thinking about things, watching the beautiful black-and-yellow birds flying about, watching the green grass balls of their nests sway.

Yes, a lot of things had gone, including Old Lucy. She'd been the last thing. That was his only justification. He'd sold everything else first: his gold cuff links, his father's watch, the silver tray. And he'd not told Helen. No good worrying her. He looked over the empty veld. Empty to him because not a head of stock on the place was his anymore. He'd rented the grazing to a butcher.

It was amazing how he missed the mare. She'd been a link with them, with Helen and her mother—with the girls. Every night she'd been waiting for him when he went to see her before he went to bed. Sometimes he'd taken a walk under the stars with her following like a dog, and now she was gone. Metz had sent a boy over for her this afternoon, and everything seemed empty and more lonely than ever.

What a difference the horse had made in his life and Helen's. That was the thing that worried him. How was he going to explain it? The mare had saved Helen. He saw that, saw that now that it was too late. It was Lucy that had given her the lift, made life worthwhile again. In every letter she asked about Old Lucy. She'd even posted a handkerchief to give to Lucy to smell. "I had it in bed all night, Daddy." He'd done it. He'd given it to Lucy, and she had looked into his face and whinnied, and now he'd sold her. For Helen, of course, and his own things had gone first, everything practically, but how was he to explain it? If only he'd told Grace about the things he'd sold. He hadn't wanted to upset her, but she'd find out when she came back. That was what always happened. One thing led to another. One lie led to the next.

He had his supper and went to bed. The frogs were croaking. There would be rain soon. He would be able to plow if he could get the time off to do it. He had not sold the tractor, thank God. But perhaps he should have; not that it would fetch much, still—it took him a long time to fall asleep. He woke suddenly. He had been dreaming of Old Lucy, dreaming he heard her.

But he was awake now, and he did hear her. Neigh after neigh. Without bothering to put on a jacket or shoes, he went out. She was there. Lucy was there, standing by the fly-netted door of the stoep.

He went out, and she almost tried to climb into his arms, as if she were a dog, as if she were saying, "I'm home again. There has been some awful mistake, but

I'm home." She forced her head between his arm and his
body. He pulled up her head and kissed her nose. I've
never kissed a horse before, he thought. But Helen has
kissed her a thousand times, has felt that soft mousy nose
with a few prickly hairs against her own lips. In a way it
was almost like kissing Helen. He took the mare for a
walk. He needed a walk. Then he watered her, put her in
the kraal with some hay.

Sleep came easier now. He was exhausted, but Old
Lucy was home. It could not last, of course. She had been
sold and paid for. The fifty pounds Metz had given him
was in the post on its way to the nursing home. Still, for
the moment God was in His heaven and Old Lucy was
home.

Frank Metz's shouts woke him. It was hardly light.
"Johnnie," he shouted, "she's here, I see."

Rubbing the sleep from his eyes, Johnnie got up. "She's
in the kraal," he said.

"I saw her."

"What happened, Frank? I was asleep when she came.
She woke me."

"I expect I woke you too."

"You did."

"Well, I had to come at once. The kids are crazy with
worry."

"What happened?"

"Happened? We put her into the kraal with mealies and
hay, and she seemed to be nicely settled. Then in the night
the kids climbed out of their windows to look at her and
found her gone. They rushed in to us yelling blue murder.
Charlie was crying."

"Did you leave the gate open, Frank?"

"Of course not. She jumped the poles—five there are, imagine it—and came straight here, straight as a crow flies."

"There are six fences between us," Johnnie said. "Barbed wire."

"I know. Imagine it. Barbed wire in the dark."

"I never heard of a horse jumping wire," Johnnie said.

"Nor have I, except in Australia. Some horses do it there. But they train them to. Hang a coat or a bag over it at first, and then make it smaller and smaller."

"Can't make a mistake with wire," Johnnie said. "Catch a foot in it and it twists. I've seen kudu caught that way."

"I know. Well, that's that. I'll leave the boy I've got with me, and he can bring her back. I'll stable her to-night."

Frank Metz got into his car and gave the boy his instructions. "Give him breakfast, Johnnie," he said. "I must get back to the kids. Pity you had your phone taken out."

That was just another of the things. I could have phoned Grace, he thought, if we still had the phone. But that would have cost money too. He looked at Frank Metz's shiny new car disappearing down the farm road and wished he was a checkbook farmer too. Still, Metz was a good guy. Very decent. If he hadn't been so decent, it would never have happened.

He'd said, "Why don't you let me have the mare, Johnnie? I'll give her a good home. Helen can see her and ride her whenever she wants." He had lit a cigarette and said, "I'll give you fifty quid for her."

That was what had done it. Just the exact figure. Just the number. He couldn't have done it with forty quid

or even sixty, though it was ten pounds more. Fifty was
the nursing-home account that had just come in the mail.
Fifty was the bull's-eye, the target.

"All right," he'd said, and never had anything been less
right. It was worse now. Old Lucy hung back in the riem,
and the boy leading her swung around and hit her with
the loose end he had in his hand.

Johnnie was beside him in a flash. Lucy was looking
at him. "Don't let him take me," she seemed to be saying.
Nonsense, he thought, a horse can't talk.

He gripped the boy's arm. "Do that again, and I'll take
the hide off you, and I'll call the *baas* when I get to town
and ask him to see if there is a mark on her." He patted
Lucy's quarters. She gave him another look and followed
the boy slowly with her nose almost on the ground.

Nothing went right that day for Johnnie. Two tractor
sales fell through. He got a flat coming home, and old
Herman met him with a long face and asked him what he
should say to the little missis when she came home. "She
loved that horse, *baas*. They used to talk together. *Ja,*
horses," he said, "talk like people. The little missis would
talk, and horse would go 'What . . . what.' " He blew
air through his nose as if he were a horse. *"Ja,"* he said,
"they talked. They talked like people."

That night Johnnie hardly slept at all. He was listening
for Lucy. He knew she couldn't come, that she was stabled.
But she came. He heard her galloping, faintly at first,
then louder and louder till the hoofbeats pulled up with
a scuffling, sliding sound below his window, and she
neighed. Not as she had last night but wildly, giving
almost a scream, the way a horse does if it's caught in a
fire. There is only one worse sound and it is the scream of

a woman. Johnnie's hair stood on end. He thought, The wire. She's hurt herself.

She was standing by the screen door still neighing when he got down. He did not even pat her, but rushed to her hind legs and ran his hands over them, from hocks to pasterns. No blood. Not a cut. Thank God, he thought, thank God. She had turned to him. Her nose was in his belly. His pajama coat was open, and he felt her warm breath. She was blowing hard. It sounded almost as if she were sobbing. Her neck was wet with sweat. So were her ears as he fondled them. He thought, Suppose she'd made a mistake and put a foot wrong. There was a bit of a moon. But suppose it had been darker. "Why didn't you come by the road?" he muttered.

She whinnied softly as if she were saying, "It's too far by road. I was in a hurry. She might be waiting for me."

I'm mad, Johnnie thought. I'm mad, thinking she said that, but he answered her all the same. He said, "I know, Lucy. It's ten miles by road and five as a crow flies." As a crow flies or a horse jumps.

That night he didn't go to bed again, but sat outside with Lucy beside him. Just before dawn she lay down as near to him as she could get. Well, this is it, he thought. Now everything is clear. He'd raise another mortgage on the farm and buy her back. I'll give Frank a hundred pounds for her, and there'll be plenty over to pay for Helen too. More than enough. He wondered why he hadn't thought of it before. He had thought of it, and then he'd stopped thinking because the interest on one bond was almost more than he could pay. But God was in this somehow—or Providence—something that was supernatural, which he felt he must not buck.

This time Frank drove up with the children. They were out before the car had stopped and rushed up to Lucy's legs. "She's not hurt, is she? She's not hurt?" they shouted.

"She's all right, Charlie," Johnnie said. "She's O.K."

The children were patting Lucy and kissing her. Charlie climbed onto her back.

"She wins," Metz said.

"I'll buy her back, Frank," Johnnie said.

"She wins, Johnnie. It's something you have to see to believe. She can stay here."

"I'll give you a hundred pounds for her," Johnnie said.

"No, no. But let's put that value on her and my kids can ride her whenever they want." He held out his hand.

And that was the way that Lucy came home.

At least the lies were over now, and Johnnie could really write to Helen about Old Lucy instead of having to invent as he had yesterday. That had been a hard letter to write with Lucy just gone. Lucy's fine. I put her to bed and went to see her before I went to sleep after dinner. What a tissue of lies. And what could he have said tomorrow if she had not come home or if she had been hurt? How could he have gone on writing?

Johnnie now began to understand the relationship his daughter had had with the old mare. Not that Lucy was old or looked old now. Helen had given her the name before she'd had her bath and beauty treatment. She had certainly looked old when he'd bought her. But she was still in her prime really. A horse was at its best at five and stayed like that till ten or more if it was looked after.

The worst was over now—even the loneliness—because he had Old Lucy to talk to. Old Herman talked to her too. Of course, they didn't really talk to the horse. They just talked, and Old Lucy cocked her ears to listen and blew out of her nostrils. She liked the sound of a human voice. But he certainly hoped it didn't get around that he was bats and talking to a horse.

A fortnight later Johnnie was holding a letter from Grace with an enclosure from Helen when Smitty came into the house with a bang that loosened the screen door on its hinges. He was smiling all over his face.

"Good news, Johnnie, very good news."

"Will she walk?"

"No, no, not yet, but she will. There's no real deterioration. They've finished all the tests. They had to wait for the reports to come back from America."

"Then?"

"Now it's just a mental block. You know the way muscles work. The nerve centers send them a message, a sort of telegram, only there's no telegraph boy for Helen. But he'll come, Johnnie, he'll come!"

Smitty was looking around the room. A lot of things had gone. Johnnie's two guns: the Purdy twelve bore and the Manlicher. So had the big silver tray that had belonged to his father. Queen Anne it was supposed to be. If he hadn't been rooked, he should have got a good price for it.

"She can come back, Johnnie. She's coming. I'm driving in to fetch them tomorrow."

He saw tears come into Johnnie's eyes. "I've missed them," he said. "Like the sun," he said. "Like days without any sun and nights without any stars. No sun, no moon, no stars. No time even. Just emptiness and silence."

"They're good girls," Smitty said. "You're a lucky man, Johnnie. One day you'll look back on all this and see what I mean. With Helen well again and Grace happy. Then you'll know the stuff that good women are made of. The guts, my boy. Helen never folded up, never gave up. Grace never complained. Not about the drought that took everything, nor Helen's illness."

"Once she got out she began to improve, Smitty. The horse was a wonderful idea."

"I'm glad you got her back."

"So you knew?"

"Everyone knew."

"It's going to be hard to tell her, Smitty."

"She'll understand. After all, you gave up everything else first."

"So you knew that too?"

"I've got eyes, and besides do you think you can send all the stuff you have away by post without there being talk? I tell you, Johnnie, your stock's up in the dorp. You'll be mayor someday if you're not careful."

"Then I'll be careful." Johnnie was laughing now. "This time tomorrow they'll be home," he said. "I must go and tell Lucy."

Smitty gave him a queer look. But he didn't care. "I talk to her," he said. "She likes it."

Smitty was laughing now. "That's what they say in the dorp. 'Johnnie's talking to that horse of his now that his wife and kid are away.'"

"Everyone talks to Lucy," Johnnie said. "The Metz kids when they come to jump her, old Herman—"

"Everyone, Johnnie? And who's everyone? Some children and a pensioned-off old Kaffir that's a bit touched in the head and you. I'll tell you something. It's a good thing to be a bit crazy like that and talk to animals. It shows a capacity for love, and that's something we're short of in the world today. You can't love a car or a tractor," he said. "You can keep them in good order. You can polish 'em and wash 'em, but you can't love 'em. People you can love if they're lovable, and animals. But love is a thing most people don't want. Though they talk about it all the time." He puffed on his pipe. "They want to be admired, to be envied, but not to be loved. To love and be loved is a responsibility.

"I'll go now," he said. He got up. "See you tomorrow when I bring them." He patted Johnnie's shoulder. "You're a good boy."

"Good boy be damned. We're the same age."

"Perhaps I'm a good boy, too, Johnnie. Who knows?"

Everything was ready for the return. The table was laid, the kettle was full of water to make them a cup of tea. He'd bought cakes in the dorp and cans of peaches that Helen liked. He'd stocked up with staples: salt, pepper, catchup, flour, sugar, tea, coffee, bacon, potatoes, butter. There was an unopened bottle of sherry on the sideboard beside the glasses. He'd put on his blue suit. Old Herman had on the clean khaki pants and shirt he'd given him. Lucy, whose riem he held, shone in the evening light.

Yes, he'd done everything that could be done. Even Grace's stoep plants had had their leaves washed. But he was still worried at the reception his news would get. I'll have to tell her. She'd find out anyway from the Metz kids or old Herman or someone. But how did one do a thing like this? How did one begin?

"They come, *baas*," old Herman shouted. "They come."

Johnnie was furious. I should have seen them first, he thought. He'd been watching the road for an hour, and the minute he looked away they came, and old Herman had seen them first.

After that things were a bit blurred for everyone—a bit choky and hard to talk. They could only kiss and hug one another. To hug Helen, Johnnie had to hug Smitty, who was carrying her, and he almost kissed him in his excitement. Lucy had come into the act and was nuzzling Helen in Smitty's arms. Old Herman had hold of Helen's foot. He could not reach her hand and was shaking it and kissing it. "The little missis," he kept saying, "the little missis."

Grace was a good girl. If she saw anything was missing in the house, she didn't say so. As a matter of fact, she saw that the silver tray had gone the minute she came in. My tray, she thought, and opened her mouth to speak. Then she saw the empty gun rack and she knew. She'd wondered all the time about money. Johnnie had never mentioned it. The visit had cost her nothing. She'd stayed with her sister Muriel and even used her car to go to the hospital, so she had never mentioned money in her letters.

She went into the kitchen to make tea and saw that Johnnie had left everything ready for her. Tears came into her eyes.

Smitty stayed on, of course. Helen sat on her father's lap. Old Herman hovered in the background and ate a piece of cake. Lucy, waiting outside, had a piece of cake. They all had sherry, and Smitty drove off.

Now's the time, Johnny thought. I'll get it over with. "Helen," he said, "did you know I sold Lucy?"

She looked at him with big sad eyes. "She's back," she said.

"I had to tell you, honey. I sold everything else first. My guns, your mother's silver tray, the cattle—"

"I must have cost a lot," Helen said.

"It was worth it. You're better."

"I'm better, Daddy. They say I'll get well. And Lucy's back."

"I had to tell you," Johnnie said.

"I knew, Daddy. Charmian wrote and told me that they had Lucy now and they loved her and would take good care of her."

"And you never wrote to me about it?"

"I think I knew why you'd done it, and then Charmian wrote again to say they didn't have her anymore, that she wouldn't stay, and how they worried about her jumping those barbed-wire fences, but that they came over and rode her here nearly every day and that now she was half theirs."

She was quiet for a moment, then she said, "We must buy her back, Daddy. I suppose they'll let us buy her back? She's mine, Daddy—ours. How can we have half a horse, and which half, which end, is ours?"

It was scarcely light next morning when Helen called her father, "Get me out, Daddy. Show me everything. Get me onto Old Lucy and lead me around."

On the veld beyond the almost empty milking kraals Helen saw the big jumps the Metz kids had put up. "Big jumps for Old Lucy," she said. "Fancy her being able to jump like that."

Johnnie said, "They love it, and she loves it. You've forgiven me?" he asked. "I sold everything else first."

"I know," she said. She could feel his big hand on her thigh. I could not feel it once, she thought. Then she said, "And now, is she theirs or ours?"

"She's half ours, darling, and half theirs. So they have riding rights too."

"They don't hurt her, do they?" Her voice was anxious. "Her mouth, I mean. Or use a whip? They never used to, of course, but the jumps are so much bigger."

"They love her," her father said.

"But she's mine, she's mine, isn't she? One day we'll pay them off, and she'll be all mine again." In her mind there was a plan forming. If Lucy can jump I'll jump her, she thought. I'll enter the show and win money. I'll tell her and she'll understand.

They went all around the farm, and then it was time for breakfast and the job.

For a month everything went on much as it had before Helen had gone to a hospital. There was no doubt about her being better. She was beginning to use her thigh muscles. She rode farther and farther every day and for longer hours. But she had an object in mind, a secret project, and one morning when her father had gone to work Helen got Herman to carry her to the kraal where the mare was munching a mixture of chaffed hay, bran, and mealies.

"Put me down," she said.

Herman set her in the soft powdered manure that covered the kraal three feet deep.

"Now," she began a conversation with the mare Lucy, "you've got to jump me. We'll jump in the show and make money and buy you back."

The mare took her head out of the manger and nibbled at her hair, spilling a mixture of chaff and mealies in it.

Herman said, "They say you can't talk to a horse, Missis." He felt the time had come to stop this.

"*Ja,* I can and do. Put her saddle on and lift me up."

"She hasn't finished her scoff yet, Missis."

"By the time you've got it on she will have." Helen reached out a hand and held the mare's foreleg below the knee. Lucy moved nearer to her.

"*Pas op,*" Herman shouted. "She'll step on you."

Helen laughed. "You couldn't make her," she said, and holding the leg pulled herself under Lucy's barrel belly. "Put the saddle on, and no bridle, just the head collar."

When the bag and surcingle were on, Helen said, "Now lift me up."

Herman lifted her.

"Now lead her to the jumps."

"No!" Herman said. "What will the *baas* say?"

"The *baas* won't know."

"And if the missis falls and breaks her neck?"

"I won't. I promise."

"*Ja,* you promise, but what about Herman? *Ja,* what about old Herman if the young missis breaks her neck?"

"Put me up," she said.

Herman lifted her up.

"Now to the jumps."

He led her there.

"Take off all the bars except the bottom one. I've got to learn, you know."

Herman took off the top three poles that the Metz children had used.

"Now, Lucy," Helen said, "take it steady."

The mare turned her ears back to listen. Helen stroked her neck and pulled herself forward. "Now," she said again, and tapped Lucy's flank with her hand.

Lucy started off at a gentle canter. When she reached the jump she went over it without hesitation, drifting over it as lightly as a leaf. She went on for twenty yards or so and came to a stop.

Helen stroked her neck and pulled her ears gently. "Good girl," she said. "Good girl." To Herman she said, "Put up the next bar."

She pulled Lucy round by her ear, and the performance was repeated. They jumped for almost an hour. Then Helen said, "Get me down now. We'll try again this evening."

When Johnnie came home he couldn't believe his eyes. Helen was jumping Old Lucy, taking her over three-foot jumps without even a bridle. And what a seat! His heart almost stopped beating and then leaped like a bird into his throat.

The mare cantered up to the jump and popped over like a buck, like a kudu. With Helen up beyond her withers, her face almost hidden in the mare's mane, her arms around her throat. Her thighs were around Lucy's neck and her legs, out of control, wobbled like those of a sawdust doll. After clearing the jump, Old Lucy slowed

up and stopped. Helen turned her by pulling on her ear.
She spoke to her and they jumped again.

Then Helen saw her father. "Hullo, Daddy," she said.
"We're jumping."

"So I see. But it's pretty high, and are you sure it's
safe?"

"Safe?" she said. "I was safe in bed when I couldn't
move. Do you want me back there?"

"No, but I still think it's high."

"We're going higher, aren't we, Lucy?" She leaned over
the mare's neck.

Lucy raised her head and neighed.

"*Magtig,*" Herman said, "*baas,* this is going on all day.
She and the little missis talk together. *Ja,*" he said, "the
horse is *tagati* (bewitched), and talks like a man. *Baas,*"
he said, "I wish to give my notice. The devil is here."

"Devil," Johnnie said. "Perhaps it is God."

"If the *baas* says so, I will stay."

Johnnie put his arms around his daughter and carried
her into the house. Old Herman and his devils! He talked
to the horse himself. Herman's notice was just a trick to
try to stop all this business in case Helen got hurt and he
was blamed.

There were new problems now for Johnnie and Grace.
Helen had the bit in her teeth. Nothing would stop her
jumping, and the mare was a natural jumper. If Helen
showed her a jump, she would clear it on her own. She'd
jumped six feet, six inches clean as a whistle that way and
come back to Helen to be petted.

"She's got something in her mind, Grace. She's not the

same girl since she came back," Johnnie said. "She's got some secret."

"And have we ever got a secret out of her?" Grace asked.

"It's not natural for a kid to be like that," Johnnie said.

"Well, she is like that, and I'm glad in a way," Grace said. "That's what'll cure her. Her will. Her iron will."

"The kid with the iron will," Johnnie said, laughing. He was proud and upset at the same time.

Next time Smitty came over they talked to him about it. "What'll we do, Smitty?"

"Let her go, Johnnie."

"Suppose she falls?"

"Suppose anyone falls," Smitty said. He put his hand on Johnnie's knee. "There's something in this that's beyond us. Call it what you like. I prefer God myself. But don't interfere. She might come right any day. Just like that. And I believe she will."

But she didn't, and she just went on jumping, with her extraordinary seat, fluttering like a bird above the cushion she still rode on.

Then it came. One evening Helen announced that she was now going to compete in the high jump at the Boomspruit stock show.

"No," Johnnie said. "I won't have it."

Helen played her trump. "Then I'll go back to bed. I won't get up." They knew she had them, and she knew too.

It was a sensation, that show. Helen Blackett's jumping was all anyone talked about. The cattle were forgotten, the harness horses, hacks, and blood horses that did their stuff in the ring were hardly looked at. Everyone was watching for the paralyzed kid. They called her paralyzed. It was good enough. Crippled, anyway.

It began with the first round. The high jump was set at four feet, and three horses failed to clear it clean before Helen and Old Lucy came on. A sort of gasp, a prolonged "Aaah" went up from the crowd when they saw the little girl with long hair on the roan mare. A kid and not even a proper saddle. No stirrups. No bridle. Only a headstall with a riem fastened under the chin. Her parents must be mad. The committee must be mad. It was a disgrace.

But the mare seemed to know what she was doing. The kid leaned forward and spoke to her. Her hands holding the riem were twisted into the mare's mane.

The horse cantered up to the jump and took off. The girl's long golden hair was flying out behind her as she left the horse's back. Her arms were around the mare's throat, her crippled legs dangling. But they were over . . . and safe. For an instant there was dead silence. Then there was a roar of approval and clapping.

It went on like that. Horse after horse was knocked out. At five feet, six inches only one other horse, a chestnut gelding, a winner at some of the bigger shows, was left in the competition. He was a big, hot-tempered beast with rolling eyes and touched the bar, knocking it off its pegs at five feet, seven inches.

Smitty and her father were standing beside Helen while she watched. "You all right?" Smitty said. He knew she was all right, more right that she'd ever been. She liked the excitement and applause.

"We can do it," was all she said. And they did. As if she knew and wanted to show off, Lucy cleared the bar with inches to spare.

Lucy got her ribbon. Helen got a cup and ten guineas prize money. Everyone congratulated her. But all she said to her father was, "That's the beginning, Daddy."

"The beginning of what, darling?"

She didn't answer. She just patted Lucy and began to cry.

That was when Mr. Lonstein came up to them. He was a fat little man who'd made a fortune with diamonds in West Africa.

"You her father?" he said to Johnnie.

"That's right," Johnnie said.

"Magnificent," Mr. Lonstein said. "Wonderful! Wonderful! She ought to jump in Johannesburg."

Helen pulled herself together. "I want to," she said. "Lucy could jump a house."

"It can't be done," her father said.

"Why not?" Mr. Lonstein asked.

"Money," her father said, "entrance fees, expenses; it just can't be done."

"I'll do it," Mr. Lonstein said. "Let me. I'll send the horse up to the city in a trailer, drive you and your daughter up in my car. A pleasure," he said. "What a day it would be. What a thrill."

"It's very kind of you," her father said, "but—"

"We'll go," Helen said. "And thank you very much."

The show was not till the fall. A lot can happen between now and then, Johnnie thought. But nothing happened except that the rains were good and his 100 acres of mealies looked wonderful, and Mr. Lonstein came down every month to see Helen and Lucy.

At first he stayed at the Jacaranda Hotel, but after a while he stayed in the house. They learned a lot about him. That he was rich they knew. That he was eccentric was obvious. That he was generous, lovable, and very funny they soon found out.

"I know what worries you, Mr. Blackett," he said. "Why should a fat little Jewish financier do this? And you're right. There must always be a motive. Well, here it is. Like I told you the first day when I met you, there's the thrill of it, the fun of it. Next there is the fact that the world should see how well Lucy jumps and Helen rides and, finally, the courage." He patted Helen's head. "Brains I've got, but no courage."

After that they took him to their hearts and loved him.

At last the great day came.

Helen and old Herman who carried her piggyback were entranced by the crowds and the livestock at the fair. Many of the beef cattle, dairy cattle, sheep, goats, horses, poultry, and rabbits were new to them. Never had they seen oxen so fat or dairy cows with such udders.

There were the usual events: a musical ride by the mounted police, the cattle parades, the hacks, the hunters, the ponies, the ladies' hacks, Thoroughbred stallions, a bayonet-fighting display by the Transvaal Scottish. The jumping—five-bar, stone wall, water jump, in and out, and the rest of them. On the third day came the high jumps with forty entries. Of them all—even the old-timers

—Helen remained calmest, and Lucy, as long as someone in the family was with her, was undisturbed by the noise or the crowd outside the ring.

As their numbers were called the riders went in.

A black gelding cleared the jump. A brown mare with a dark girl tipped the bar. A gray cleared it. A bay Thoroughbred came next, cleared it, and almost ran away when he landed.

Helen was next. Mr. Lonstein led her out and let go. Once again there was a hush. Fancy a kid like that competing with adults. . . . The horse looks all right, but—

That was when Lucy started for the jump. No saddle, no proper bridle . . . a crippled girl. How could they? But there she was, going at it.

Old Lucy cocked her ears and slowed her canter. Helen pulled herself forward by her mane, climbing the mare's mane like a monkey on a stick, as Lucy dug her heels into the ground and shot forward.

"She's off!" someone shouted. But they were wrong. And the mare was over.

Helen jumped twice more that day, and each time it was the same. She was watched with a sort of horrified silence that was followed by a roar of approval.

That night the *Star* had headlines:

Crippled Girl Jumps

Miss Helen Blackett, of Boomspruit, has no strength in her legs, which are crippled, and has developed a style of jumping that brings the hearts of all who watch her into their mouths but gets her over.

Mr. Lonstein was jubilant. "Oh, the fun of it," he said,

and took them all out to dinner. Helen was a heroine, but she took it calmly. There was only one thing in her mind: the prize money, a hundred guineas this time, and nothing was going to stop her.

"Then you'll be mine," she whispered to Lucy, "all mine, not the front half or the back half, but all of you . . . all . . . every bit."

Her mother looked at her and wondered about her. The child wasn't smiling. She wasn't proud. She just seemed preoccupied. Her mouth was a thin, hard line, her little chin stuck out. Her eyes were cold. She was polite to everyone, but no more.

Her dear lovable little Helen had gone. This was a determined girl. What was it she wanted? Kudos? Praise? Adulation? She didn't seem to. Her mother knew she meant to win.

What she did not know was how frightened Helen was. Only Mr. Lonstein knew, because he was so easily made afraid himself. He'd known the first time he saw her in Boomspruit. That was what he had admired so much. This was real courage. Any fool with no brains could be brave, but she was smart enough to be afraid and strong enough to overcome her fear, a kid like that. But he did not know that what she said to herself each time she came up to a jump was, "Throw your heart over, Helen," and that in her mind she threw it up over the jump like a ball as Old Lucy took off.

In the finals there were only three entries left: a young Englishman riding a gray Irish hunter, a Johannesburg girl riding a bay mare called Kitty, and Helen. The Irish hunter failed at five feet, ten inches. He cleared it but, being a chaser, was careless and hit the pole with his near hind hoof. That put him out. Both the girl on the bay and Helen cleared it.

The girl said, "Funny us both being girls and riding mares."

Helen said, "Yes," but didn't think it funny.

The girl was slim and beautiful and could ride. The bay mare was beautiful. The girl's saddlery and gear were beautiful. The girl's jacket and breeches were beautiful. Her boots were beautiful. Her long slim thighs that gripped the beautiful saddle on the beautiful bay mare were beautiful. Helen hated her.

There was only this girl between her and the half of Lucy she did not own. She thought she could have killed her; at least she understood now why people were killed; they were too beautiful. All those actresses that were murdered in the Sunday papers.

She patted Lucy's neck.

Five feet, eleven inches. It was the girl again. Her name was listed as Georgina Haslett, but she was just *the* girl to Helen. The girl cleared it. Helen cleared it. Two men put up the pegs another notch—six feet.

"You take it," the girl said. "My girth needs fixing."

Someone shouted to the judge. He shouted back. A man ran up to explain. He put his mouth to the mike. "Her name is Miss Helen Blackett," came over the air as if God had shouted it.

The girl, Helen thought. She's afraid. There's nothing wrong with her girth. And I'm afraid. Six feet was so high. As high as Daddy. Much, much more than an inch higher than five feet, eleven inches. She tried to remember the world's record jump: six feet, six inches. Only six inches more.

Lucy was cantering slowly toward the two black-and-white posts that supported the bar. The closer they got, the higher it seemed to Helen. Then her courage came back. "It's for you, Lucy," she said.

The mare laid one ear back to listen. Then she cocked it forward and switched her tail. She seemed to think this was fun. This was real jumping. She slowed up a little as she felt Helen climbing up her neck.

"N-n-now," Helen shouted. "Now, Lucy!" and they were off. One—two great bounds that were almost leaps and they were airborne.

Helen came right up higher than Lucy's head. She could look down on her forehead and the star. She noticed the way her forelock, divided into two as usual, was blowing back. She saw the white faces of the people in the grandstand, and then she slid back. They had done it. She patted Lucy and the crowd roared.

Now let her try, Helen thought. Let that girl and her damn bay mare do it. She was surprised at herself. She had never said "damn" before.

But the girl did not do it. She was afraid, and the mare knew it. The bay never even came up, but struck the bar with her chest.

Everyone was around them now: Daddy and Mother and Smitty and old Herman and Mr. Lonstein. They all went up with her, like a deputation, to get her cup, the check in an envelope, and a blue ribbon for Lucy.

She'd done it. It was over.

"You're famous," someone said.

"Fancy a kid winning the Rand Show high jump!" But Helen hardly heard them. What she did hear was Smitty, who said, "I've got crutches for you, Helen. I'm sure you can use them now," and he slipped them under her arms as he helped her down from the horse. He held her till she got her balance, and she found she could use them. Her left leg would support her if someone held her belt.

They stayed two more days. Her left leg could support her. The right was still weak, but she could get about on her own and had seen most of the show again. Everyone knew her and liked her. Most of them had seen her jump Old Lucy.

She was eating an ice-cream cone when a stableboy ran up to her. She knew him well by sight, a boy called Franz. He looked after two other jumpers.

"Missis! Missis!" he shouted. "Come quick. The man," he said. "*Ja,* the *baas,* he's trying to jump her and she won't. Then he hit her with his *sjambok.*"

Helen looked at him wide-eyed, wiping the ice cream from her mouth. "Jumping? Jumping who?"

"*Die missis se perd,*" he said. "Your horse, Old Lucy. Man he struck her, and your boy is killed."

Before he had finished Helen was off, hopping toward the practice jumps like a wounded rabbit. A man trying to jump Old Lucy. Her man was dead. He had tried to stop it. The man had hit him. He hit Lucy.

The blood boiled in her veins. Suddenly she knew that she had never been angry in her life before. Not like this. I said damn, she thought. She said it again. Damn him! Damn him! A murderer! Beating Old Lucy, and old Herman dead!

He— She increased her pace. Coming around the side of the stables, she saw him: a big redheaded young man on Old Lucy's back, trying to force her over a jump that she had refused. Her mouth was bleeding from the heavy bit he had put into her mouth, and she had a curd of froth and foam on her chest.

"I'll teach you," he said. *"Ja,* you damn lazy *skelm."* He raised his whip and brought it down on Old Lucy's quarters. She laid her ears back and showed the whites of her eyes, but did not move. The man jumped off, holding the riem in his hands, and began to thrash the mare.

Without knowing how she did it, Helen was running. She had let one crutch fall and charged the man, using the other like a bayonet. She struck the man in the side. As he turned to face her, Old Lucy pulled free and swung around to her mistress's side.

"What the hell!" the man shouted.

"My horse," Helen hissed at him. "You dared to hit my horse. And my boy." Old Herman was not dead. He hobbled toward her.

"I was just teaching her," the man said. "A horse must learn to respect a man—a woman too. *Magtig,* never has a woman struck me. Never before—"

He did not finish. The crutch point took him in the throat. He went down, and Helen beat at him as if he were a snake.

He got up and tried to seize her arm. Old Lucy chopped at him. Then with a flash of teeth and flaring nostrils she took him by the collar of his coat and shook him like a rat.

By now a crowd was around them, white and black, visitors, owners, grooms.

"Like a bloody rat," a man said. "I've heard a horse could lift a man in his teeth, but I've never seen it."

Helen was sobbing, with her arms around Old Lucy's neck. Old Herman was patting her shoulder. "Drunk," he

said. "*Ja,* he was drunk. I tried to stop him, and he hit me
flat."

It was all a nightmare, a dream. It wasn't true. The
mare pushed her nose into her chest. Helen pulled her
ears and rubbed her poll, kneading it with her fingers.
Then she looked down and saw her crutch on the ground.
It had been broken in the scuffle.

What'll I do? she thought. How will I get about, and
where is the other one? Then it dawned on her. She was
standing. She had run. She had fought a man. She had
won a hundred guineas and could buy Lucy back. I can
walk, she thought, and Lucy's mine. That she had won a
great competition was forgotten. The little Helen that her
mother loved was back.

Helen was standing crying bitterly, her arms wound
around her horse's neck, when Grace and Johnnie found
her.

LAST BRONC
Colin Lofting

As Eric Gordon clambered up the side of the gate he could feel the dull pain in his left knee. He reached over and uncoiled the bronc rein from the top plank of the chute. For a moment he studied the horse's mean, small eye. A feeling of apprehension made him wriggle his shoulders; the bronc's eye rolled back, showing a lot of white.

He held the rein back over the swell of the saddle as if he were a salesman measuring cloth. When he'd found the exact length of the hold he planned to take, he pulled a hank of hair from the bronc's mane and knotted it around the rope where he wanted to grasp with his left hand. By doing this he would be in the chute less time and he could save his knee. He crawled down to the ground and hunkered in the shade of the chute, waiting for his turn to ride.

Well, this was it. This was the last one. Funny, a man could measure his life in a series of bronc rides. Take the first time; he was eleven. The new hired man had jumped on one of the workhorses and was promptly bucked off. Two days later when he thought no one had been watching the round corral back of the barn, he saddled the old mare in the crowding pen and then kicked the gate open. She squealed once and lumbered out into the corral, sending up clouds of dust. He tried to look like the pictures he'd seen in the papers: his right hand held free, his feet arching high on every jump. He remembered the scared feeling he had when suddenly he was out of breath and his vision blurred. He hadn't realized it was so rough. The old mare, fortunately, tired as quickly as he did, and she stood still in the center of the corral, her sides heaving rhythmically.

Then he heard the clatter of hands clapping. It was Elinore, a freckle-faced kid he'd known all his life. Her family owned the ranch to the north. He was scared she would tell his dad. When he'd caught his breath he made her promise, and cross her heart, not to tell a soul.

A horse with a reputation was a nagging, relentless challenge. He traveled miles from home just to ride a horse that had bucked others off. One summer he worked for a man who bought bucking stock and by the time he went to college he was a natural on the rodeo team.

Intercollegiate champion. While he stood there in the glaring lights of the Cow Palace, receiving a hand-tooled saddle amidst the popping photographers' flashbulbs, it was the happiest moment of his life.

His dad and mom had seen the finals, and after the show he'd been surprised and then a little ashamed because they had brought the skinny Elinore along with them. He had to pose with the rodeo queen, a tall, curvaceous blonde. Elinore then had seemed like such a kid.

Perhaps the rest had been too easy. He turned professional and burned up the circuit like a prairie fire. He was lucky as well as good; he drew the kind of horses he rode best, and his second year, after graduating from college, he was the world's champion cowboy. They awarded the title on the basis of a point for every dollar won, and the dollars were a good enough excuse then. He wondered why he needed an excuse; certainly he sent more money home than his folks had ever dreamed he could make contesting, but the few times he had been home he'd felt uncomfortable. Sitting on the veranda after supper and listening to the talk of crops, cattle, and weather would get on his nerves, and he'd long for the crowded hotel rooms, the card games, and the moving life of traveling from one show to the next.

Now his mind heard the announcer's words, "Sonny Grebb coming out of Chute Number Five on Suicide Sid."

Eric turned and watched the gate to Number Five. Sonny Grebb was a comer, one of those crowd-pleasing, easy riders who made a fetish out of every move, every move a thing of easy grace. He wanted desperately to beat Sonny; it was strange how the idea had grown from a natural competitive desire to an obsession. Perhaps Sonny exemplified his own lost ability and accentuated his failing courage.

The bronc ran a few strides and then savagely bogged his head. Eric watched the clever way Sonny did all his scoring in the air and had his feet set each time the spine-jarring horse hit the ground. It was a good ride, and as Sonny vaulted over the rump of the pickup man's horse, the crowd gave him a sincere ovation. Sonny acknowl-edged the clapping and whistling by a modest doff of his hat as he took little running steps back to the chute.

Eric thought, Wait, kid, just wait until you lose the bounce. Wait until the injuries pile up.

Someone touched his shoulder. He looked up into the drawn face of Bill Decker. Bill made a little motion with his head toward the back of the chutes and touched a bulge in his shirtfront above his belt.

"No, no thanks, Bill," Eric said quietly.

Well, there you had both ends of the road: Sonny about to bask in thunderous applause for a few years, and poor old Bill, the ever-present pint in his shirt hoping to luck up on an easy horse and make enough money to enter another show, money for another cheap hotel room and another pint.

Eric rose stiffly to his feet and lit a cigarette. He wished there weren't so many entries in the saddle-bronc riding. He'd like to get his own ride over with and get away from the show. He was a darn fool to come to Prescott; the very best were there. He should duck riders like Sonny Grebb, pick up a little money at the smaller shows or go home.

He'd known, for a year, it was time to quit. Lately he hardly sent home the wages of a top cowhand. He could have sent home more; he couldn't afford the last car. He could have bunked in the smaller hotels.

Suddenly he wished he had accepted Bill's offer and

had a drink. He felt an unnatural moisture in the lines of the palms. He wiped his hands on the knees of his chaps. He realized his nerve was a dying thing. Perhaps one more fall or seeing someone else badly hurt would be the end, and then he remembered this was to be his last ride.

He had made up his mind a month ago. When he was turning into the family's lane, sudden nostalgia had swept over him.

Climbing out of his big car, he tried to hide his lameness, but his mother, running down the wide veranda stairs, said, "Oh, Eric, what have you done now?"

"Nothing, Mom, really. Rammed into a pickup man's horse. It'll be all right."

As he spoke he thought of the many times he'd repeated the words, from the time he was a little shaver until now.

Mom put her hands on his upper arms and stared into his eyes. "Is everything all right, Son?"

Mom could make him feel bad when she asked a question like that; he knew that she knew. "Sure, Mom; everything's fine."

He followed her into the big room. Dad came out of the office, and he looked older and thinner. He shook Eric's hand, his eyes searching Eric's face.

Eric cleared his throat awkwardly and asked, "How's the new bunch of heifers doing?" and as he spoke, the words rang insincerely in his ears.

"Good. They're fine. Must have calved out better than ninety percent," his dad answered, hesitating as if he wanted to say more; then he turned and went back to his rolltop desk.

Eric turned and looked around the familiar room. There

were many pictures of himself—riding broncs, lined up
with other winners at a big show, and a few taken for
cigarette and overall advertisements.

"Dinner will be ready soon, Son. Elinore's coming
over," his mother said quietly.

While he shaved he noticed the almost permanent lines
of a wince around his eyes. He lay soaking in a tub, the
water as hot as he could stand it, and he thought of the
entry blanks in his suitcase. He only had a day or two to
make up his mind. He could duck the senior circuit and
swing through the Northwest, hitting the smaller shows.
But he knew he wouldn't. No, he'd compete once again
with the best.

He went downstairs and sat in the big chair by the window. When he heard Elinore's steps on the porch, he rose
stiffly.

She hesitated, her hand on the screen door. She hadn't
seen him. He felt a sudden contraction of his muscles.
She had changed; now she was a woman. She turned for
a moment and looked off across the front pasture. Then
she straightened her shoulders and came into the room.
She blushed when she saw him, and he realized that she
thought she had been alone.

Taking both his hands in hers, she said, "It's good to
see you. It's been a long time."

Her hands felt strong and warm. She squeezed his and
let them drop. "How do you think your family looks?"
she asked, and Eric sensed an importance beneath her con-
versational tone.

"Fine. Dad's a little thin lookin' and—" His voice
stumbled to silence as he thought of the logical answer
to that; he knew his dad worked too hard.

Just then Mom came into the room. She kissed Elinore's cheek and said, "Dinner's on."

Perhaps it was the set pattern that irritated him; he knew, before each thing happened, just what would take place. He and his father went onto the porch while Mom and Elinore did the dishes. His father lit his pipe, and Eric expected him to talk about ranching, but for a long moment his father was silent; then he got to his feet and stood near Eric's chair.

"I have to go to town, some stockmen's meeting. You're going to be around awhile?"

"I don't know which show I'll take in next, but I'll be here a day or two anyway."

His dad started to move, and then stopped. "You know, Son, I wanted to enlist right after Pearl Harbor. I couldn't leave the ranch."

Eric knew why his father told him this. Before he could think of anything to say, his dad left the veranda. Eric heard the car leave the garage.

It was the edge of dark; his mother and Elinore joined him. Soon the rhythmic creak of the swinging settee joined the gentle noises of the night.

He hardly heard the small talk; he answered mechanically. His mind heard the noises of the arena: the bawling of stock; the creaking, grunting noise of an exploding bronc; the shouts and laughter around the chutes; the band in the grandstand, and the intruding chant of the vendors hawking their wares.

His mother excused herself, and Eric felt the pain in his knee as he got to his feet while she went into the house.

"Have you seen a doctor?" Elinore asked, hardly above a whisper.

"There's nothing broken," he answered evasively, because he hadn't seen a doctor; he knew what a doctor would tell him. Sometimes he thought everyone wanted the chance to tell him it was time to quit.

He glanced at Elinore, leaning against a post on the rail of the veranda. He could hardly believe that she could have changed so much since he'd seen her last.

He went to the door and turned the porch light off. "Darn bugs'll carry you off," he mumbled in explanation. He came over near Elinore and sat down on the railing. Her nearness slowly spread over him, and he could feel a nerve fluttering at the base of his throat.

He hardly thought of what he was doing; the sudden desire overwhelmed him. Before he'd realized the crude insistency of his actions, he had pulled Elinore toward him and was kissing her. When she returned his kiss, happiness welled up within him until he wanted to shout. The doubts and fears of the last year dropped from him. Then he felt Elinore stiffen in his arms.

"Why did you do that?" she asked, her frankly curious voice reminding him of the freckle-faced kid he used to fish with.

He didn't know what to say; he didn't want to lose her, and yet couldn't talk about himself. She and his family would never understand. "I don't know," he mumbled.

She took a step backward, and he could feel her glance searching his face. "Your dad needs you on the place. You'll hate me for telling you, but it's time someone shared the responsibility."

"I'm going to hang up after Prescott," he said, realizing he'd made the decision that very instant.

"Wouldn't it be easier to just—not go back?"

How could you explain that you wanted to ride just one the way you used to? And how could you put into words your desire to beat Sonny? You'd pretended it was all for money, but there was something else, something far stronger than cold cash. You couldn't explain that three days ago you had pulled leather. On the third jump you'd almost gone, and without realizing it your right hand had clamped onto the horn of the saddle with a death grip. When you went back to the chute, there wasn't the usual kidding; most of the contestants found an excuse to turn away; a saddle needed to be moved or a spur strap needed tightening. No, it was no use trying to explain.

When he didn't answer, she suddenly stepped forward and kissed the cleft in his chin. "Good night," she said, and her voice quavered.

Before he could find words, she'd turned and left the veranda. He watched her shadow melt into cottonwoods by the creek. For a moment he thought of following her; then he remembered the barrier of not being able to explain.

He sat there, wishing he hadn't said he would quit. He sat there until he saw the lights of his father's car. Then he went to his room. He had left home early the following morning.

Now the announcer's voice penetrated Eric's thoughts, "Coming out of Chute Number Two, Bill Decker on Dillinger!"

He turned and saw Bill's drawn face as he lowered himself onto the bronc. Bill's eyes were glazed, and as he wriggled himself deep into the saddle his head lolled. The gate swung open and from the very first jump it was a pitiful sight. Bill had had a few drinks too many, and he reminded Eric of a gunny sack being worried by a dog.

Eric found himself hobbling out into the arena with the others; they knew it was a matter of seconds. They watched helplessly. The bronc seemed to relish the loose burden on his back; he squealed like a pig and kicked viciously at the top of each crooked jump. Bill went over the bronc's neck just as the bronc threw up his head. Bill's head snapped back, and Eric saw a crimson blotch above his eye as the man seemed to be suspended in midair. Then Bill crumpled into the arena's dust, face downward.

They turned him over gently, and Eric wondered if the others smelled the fetid odor of stale alcohol. He followed the knot of men who carried the limp body back to the chutes. He knew that someone should pass the hat this afternoon, because Bill wouldn't be traveling on to the next show.

Sonny Grebb was walking next to him. "Woof, that was rough. When I was a kid, that man was my idea of hell on wheels."

Eric shot a glance at the handsome face, suddenly serious and lost in thought. "He was a skookum hand, all right," Eric said. Then he added, "Here's twenty dollars. You've ridden your horse; you have time. How about seein' what you can raise for Bill?"

Sonny said, hesitating, "I'm lucky now, Eric, and you're not going—your knee's giving you hell. Why don't you—" Sonny's voice stumbled to quiet as he realized the implication. He took the money, and reaching for his own wallet he turned, leaving Eric alone.

Only three more horses and then it was his turn to ride.

He watched the next bronc, and the mere waiting made the ten-second ride seem an eternity.

The next bronc came out and turned suddenly to the right. The riders in front of the chute scattered to the fence as if they were frightened. Suddenly the bronc started to fall; he'd crossed his front legs and the momentum of his bucking carried him forward, giving him no chance to regain his balance.

Eric closed his eyes, but the roar of the crowd suddenly changing from wild cheering to an awe-struck gasp of horror made him open them against his will. The belly of the fallen bronc was toward him, and under the cinch, pressed into the ground, he saw the rider's foot still in the stirrup. He turned as the horse struggled to his feet. He felt something brush the short hairs on the nape of his neck, and a shiver passed down his spine.

He thought of Elinore. It was now a month since last he'd seen her. In each hotel he would glance in the mailbox behind the desk whenever he'd asked for his key. But there never had been a letter. Well, he didn't blame her. He'd written once, just a note saying he'd be home after Prescott, and then he'd wondered why she would be interested. She probably thought he was pretty conceited to write. And yet, when he thought of the last time he'd seen her, he was filled with yearning. Several times he'd found himself searching the sea of faces in the grandstand but why should she—

While the last bronc before his ride was still in the arena, Eric started up the side of the chute. Sonny Grebb appeared on the other side, one leg hooked over the top plank.

"I got over two hundred dollars for Bill," he said casually. Then he pulled a small bag of resin from his pocket and handed it to Eric. Eric wiped his hands on it and tossed it back.

"Know anything about this horse?" Eric asked.

Sonny looked down in the chute. "No, they didn't use him in the first go-rounds."

It was on the tip of his tongue to tell Sonny that this was his last ride, but he didn't. He took up the belt of his chaps another hole and rested, waiting for the announcer. He was glad to find that he felt the same way he used to, now that he was on the chute—calm and cool.

There it was: "Coming out of Chute Number Five, the former world's champion cowboy, Eric Gordon, on the Bitterroot Bomb."

He felt Sonny's hand steadying him, holding the belt of his chaps as he straddled the inside of the chute and climbed down into the saddle. He found the knot of horsehair on the rein with his left hand. He tugged his hat down and worked his feet into the stirrups.

"Turn me outta here," he said to the man behind the gate.

From the very first jump, he sensed something was wrong. The bronc was panicky, and at the top of each jump he'd kick out to one side, bringing his hoofs close to the flank strap and then lashing out viciously. Each time Eric wondered if the horse would get his feet under him in time to stay upright when he hit the ground. Then it happened; the horse landed with all his weight on his near front leg. For a full second the bronc seemed to balance, and then he crumpled as if he'd been shot.

Now Eric saw the veins inside the extended nostril, and

then, when the horse expelled his breath with a roar, there was a puff of dust. He realized he was prone, dangerously close to the fallen animal, and he should move before the horse scrambled to his feet, but his own limbs wouldn't answer. Then he felt their hands pulling him away.

Things appeared to be fuzzy, and Sonny's face floated back and forth, reminding Eric of someone adjusting a movie projector.

"Never seen you go better! If that pig had kept his feet, you'd have had yourself a scoring ride!" Sonny's voice was excited.

Everett Bowman, one of the judges, rode up and said, "You're the only reride. We'll send you out after the calf-roping finals, if you're all right."

Before Eric could answer, Bowman rode off.

Reride! For some reason he hadn't thought of that. Yes, his horse had fallen with him, and he was entitled to another ride. Suddenly fear swept over him, and he felt the ooze of sweat between his shoulder blades.

"You all right?" Sonny asked.

"Yeah, I seem to be," he answered, and then was instantly sorry he had spoken, because something—something he didn't understand—told him he wouldn't take his reride. It would have been better to say that something felt broken.

He hobbled over to the chute and leaned against the whitewashed planks. He wanted to tell someone, anyone, but he couldn't talk about it. This was what he'd been afraid of for a year; he'd been afraid of losing his nerve. It hadn't been a fear of getting hurt as much as it was the fear of what the others would think. This was what he'd dreaded.

He looked up at the judges' stand, the small towerlike pavilion above the chutes. He'd have to go up there and tell them he couldn't take his reride. He saw Cy Morgan, the announcer, pick up the mike, and then Cy's voice crackled over the grounds, announcing the finals of the calf roping.

He stood there alone, and he could feel the dampness chilling along his spine. He turned, wondering if the other riders were watching him. He glanced both ways; most of the bronc riders were waiting to watch the roping. He saw Sonny Grebb tying his bronc rein around his rolled chaps. He heard someone hazing a horse into the chutes, and with a feeling of panic he realized it was his bronc.

"Hey, Sonny!" he called.

Sonny came over to him.

"Sonny, do me a favor? Go on up, and tell 'em I'm not riding."

Sonny gave him a long, searching stare. Eric wondered if it were his imagination, because he thought he saw the trace of a sneer flick the corner of Sonny's mouth just before he turned and headed for the stairs to the stand.

He felt incredibly tired. He hardly saw the calf roping. He wanted to leave, but the last show of courage he could display to himself was to stay until the end of the show. He dreaded the customary gabfest where everybody said good-by and chatted about who'd be going where next. But he'd wait. And in a way he wanted to say good-by to the other contestants.

The calf roping was over. He wondered where Sonny had gone, and then he thought Sonny was probably embarrassed to be with him. Suddenly he started violently because he heard his own name on the public-address system.

"Eric Gordon, one of the greatest bronc riders and one of the most popular cowboys of our time! He'll be coming out of Chute Number Five on Ground Loop for his reride! Let's give this rider a big hand! We have learned that this is to be Eric Gordon's last show!"

Panic clutched at him, and yet he stood up mechanically and fastened the snaps to his chaps. His mind could hardly keep up to his actions. He knew the crowd was waiting. He wondered what had happened to Sonny, why he hadn't told them in the stands.

He headed for Number Five. Sonny leaned over the gate and called, "Hurry up! I got your riggin' on just right!"

Eric looked up and saw the sheepish grin on Sonny's face. He started up the outside of the gate. Suddenly he wondered who could have told the announcer that this was to be his last show. He tried to remember telling anybody, but he'd only mentioned it once.

He went down onto the bronc, Sonny's hand holding the belt of his chaps. He tested the length of his hold and wriggled deep into the saddle.

Sonny took some gum from his mouth and stuck it in the bronc's mane behind his ears. "Kick that loose for me, champ."

He waited a second. Because he was so surprised and hurried, he realized he was out of breath. The arena was as quiet as a tomb. His own voice sounded loud, "Turn him out."

After the second jump, he knew he had a good horse.

In spite of the pain in his knee, he kicked high in front of the crest of each buck and then brought his feet back, almost hitting the cantle of the saddle. The horse was rough, but Eric suddenly felt at home. He eased off on his hold, and his left hand moved freely, almost disdainfully. His face felt strange, and then he realized he was grinning. Just before the gun went off, he heard his own whoop echo across the arena. He kept on contesting until he saw the pickup man's horse next to him.

For a moment he thought there'd been an accident, because the men from around the chute were all in the arena, and then he realized they were coming to meet him. He felt happy pride well up within him as, one by one, they came and shook his hand. The band played a march and he could hear the scuffle of feet as the crowd left the stands. While he was shaking hands and saying "good-by," his mind kept asking one question.

Everett Bowman rode up and shook his hand. "Can't remember giving more points on one ride. We'll remember that one. You won day money easy."

"Thanks, Ev. Thanks a lot," he mumbled.

He kept looking for Sonny, and then he saw him over near the chutes, talking to a girl. And then he had his answer: the girl was Elinore.

When he reached them, Sonny shook his hand. "I bet that gum got knocked off. Only hope I got sense enough to quit on top. Sense enough and a gal who—" Sonny stopped abruptly. "I'll see you soon, Eric, on your ranch." He turned and joined the leaving crowd.

Eric searched her eyes. He saw that they were moist, but she was smiling. "Will you ever forgive me?" she asked.

"Forgive you! I'll never be able to thank you. Do you know what it would have been like to quit, not taking my reride?"

"You won't give me credit for knowing you at all," she said, and beneath her bantering tone Eric sensed a veiled seriousness.

As it slowly dawned on him what she had done, a feeling of doubt left him. What went on inside a man might be unimportant, but if his—suddenly Eric checked his thoughts; perhaps he was getting ahead of himself.

"I heard Sonny Grebb say he was going to give you a five-minute rest, and then ask you again if you didn't want to take your reride. That's when I told them it was your last show. I told them you wouldn't ride again because you'd promised me."

"You believed me?" he asked.

"I've believed you all my life."

He stood there, smiling foolishly. She stepped toward him and touched his arm with her fingertips. Hardly above a whisper, she said, "Please take me where you can kiss me, and then let's start—start home."

He turned and looked at the shadow of the stand in the fading light. The setting sun tinged the spirals of dust a crimson color. The impatient honking of car horns, leaving the parking area, mingled with the shouts of men putting the show stock back in their pens. Suddenly he realized how very much he loved this girl. He turned and looked into her eyes.

"I can't wait," she said, stepping into his arms.

LANKO'S WHITE MARE
H. E. Bates

Every morning just after daybreak Lanko, the quoits man, led out the white mare along with the other horses from the fair and watered her. Every day she was a conspicuous figure, the only white one in a long line of handsome grays, chestnuts, blacks, and piebalds, the only one old, patient, and slow.

On Lanko's head there were white hairs too, and he also in spite of his flashing dark eyes was slow and steady when he walked. He and the mare never went too fast for each other, and he never grew impatient with her. On the contrary he understood her perfectly, trusting her to walk wherever he wished merely by a touch on her side. And she too knew this touch unmistakably, because he had given it her with the same unfailing gentleness and care for nearly fifteen years.

One morning, in order to be ready to depart with the rest, Lanko was in a hurry to get back to the fairground. He was a little farther behind the other horses than usual. In the fairground itself, ever since before dawn, there had been commotion: the rattling of buckets, shrill voices, the jingle of harness, the heavy cough of great engines making their steam. Coming out of the gates, Lanko had had an argument with the Fat Lady man, an argument completely trivial and foolish, but one which nevertheless had aroused a spark of anger in his eyes and had thrown him behind the rest.

For the first time when taking the white mare to drink he felt impatient; in the chilly morning air, with the sounds of departure behind him and the clatter of hoofs in front, the distance to the drinking place seemed to him tremendous. He knew that the white mare did not understand this. Her pace did not once quicken; she did not notice the absence of her fellow creatures. Yet he felt that because she had been understanding and obedient for nearly fifteen years she must understand now.

"We're late!" he told her. He slapped her ribs.

Her pace did not alter. It was as if this unexpected touch had plunged her into a state of puzzled wonder in which she could not obey.

She kept steadily onward. After a moment Lanko ran a little in front of her and beckoned her, pulling the halter gently. She seemed to recognize his presence, but without responding, without increasing her pace even a little. He began to run at her side, slapping her ribs again, as if to encourage her to imitate him. But she would not run, would not disturb herself, would not even turn her head.

Lanko began to grow puzzled. A little more than half-way to the drinking place he saw the rest of the horses begin to return. This had not ever happened before; he had been there, day after day for fifteen years, with the rest. Now he would be forced to meet them returning, would have to stand aside while the handsome, many-colored crowd cantered past. In his mood of half disappointment, half consternation, he even desisted from urging the mare onward, and they fell into their habitual pace again, neither one too fast for the other, as if their patient and mutual understanding had suffered no break.

In a moment the long line of blacks and piebalds, roans and browns began to trot past him. He awoke from his mood of disappointment. He was only impatient and ashamed as he drew the white mare to the roadside, holding her there while the rest cantered disdainfully past, the men flaunting their arms, whistling and shouting, demanding what had become of him in a good-natured tirade that he could not understand. It seemed to him an hour before the mass of clattering hoofs filed past; he had not thought before that so many horses could come from the fair.

The last of the men, suddenly distasteful and aggravating to him in their red-and-check shirts, shouted, "She's only a filly! Make her gallop! You'll never get away!" They turned on the bare backs of their horses and laughed at him.

Their reproaches stung him. With sudden anger he struck the mare's ribs again. It was a blow under which he had expected her to leap forward, as if startled by a shot. Instead she moved onward slowly, patient and steady, with the habitual faith and obedience of fifteen years. Enraged by this, Lanko ran before and behind her, entreating, urging, beckoning her, pulling her halter, striking her ribs with even heavier blows than before, but without ever inducing her to change her pace. He pulled at her head and glared into her eyes. They seemed to him suddenly unintelligent, sleepy and stupid.

Like this he managed to get her to the drinking pool at last, leading her down to the edge by the halter, pulling down her head until it touched the water. This was his every morning custom, a gesture of tender assistance, as toward a child. The white mare always responded, always drank her fill. But on this morning she only sniffed the water, gazed downward as if at her own reflection in the surface, then lifted her head and turned away.

Lanko was puzzled. The pool was muddy from the feet of the other horses, but he had seen her drink during fifteen years the foulest and most stagnant of waters. She too had suffered hardships. He patted her head in understanding of this. In a moment she would drink, he thought, if only he were patient, if only he waited.

For nearly a minute he was true to this resolve; he stood caressing the silk of her nostrils as he had so often done, humoring her, talking to her, full of patience for her. But she did not drink. All the time her head dropped a little toward the water, as if she were making up her mind, as if she were dreaming. The ripples her feet had made in the surface ran far away, grew faint, and then died, she remained so still.

"Drink! For God's sake, drink, and let's get away!"

His words were half command, half entreaty. But she did not move, though it seemed to him she must under-

stand why he had brought her there, simply because for
fifteen years, morning by morning, she had understood
and obeyed.

Lanko grew desperate again. "Drink!" He slapped her
ribs. It was as if she were dead to all feeling; she did not
respond, did not even quiver.

"Drink! Damn you, drink!" he shouted suddenly. He
pulled down her head to the water again, wetting her lips.
Without even a mouthful she raised it again and turned
away.

He led her to another part of the pool and repeated the
gesture to which she had never failed to respond, sup-
pressing momentarily all impatience and anger. But there,
as before, he drew from her only the response, as it
seemed to him, of a stupid and stubborn will.

His anger grew uncontrollable; he wrenched the halter
upward and from the bank dragged at the white mare's
head until she followed him. "If you won't drink you must
go thirsty, damn you!"

Suddenly he thought, I shall be last. They'll be har-
nessed up and gone. I shall be crowded out.

This, he thought fiercely, had never happened, and for
the sake of a mare that wouldn't drink, never should! He
shouted to the mare, threatening her.

The mare remained still, staring emptily ahead. Lanko
turned and looked at her, and then, angered by this long
succession of futile words, of unanswered gestures and
tenderness, strode forward and with his uplifted knee
kicked her in the ribs.

There was a pause. Then Lanko, though able to see how
startled she was, how deeply she felt the blow, pushed her
hindquarters desperately. To his immense relief she re-

sponded and began to move off. But she seemed slower
even than usual, heavier in body; her feet touched the
ground uncertainly, her head had drooped a little.

It began to be urged upon Lanko very slowly, in spite
of his joy at seeing her move again, that his difficulties
with her were not ended. Matters grew worse as he re-
called the mornings when she had trotted back from
drinking, when the longest journeys in summer had not
seemed to tire her.

As they went back he tried to put down her lethargy
to a sudden fit of laziness or caprice. But it did not ease
his mind, only his anger abated a little, and he walked
at her side with all his old patience, exactly in time with
her, patting her side gently in order to remind her of his
presence.

Some caravans were already leaving the fairground as
he arrived there. It was a relief to find that he would not
be crowded out; looking at the sky he thought he would
be away before the sun was far up.

The white mare stood very still while he fetched her
harness. This morning, as always before, he dropped it
over her back with practised quickness and ease, with a
great jingle of buckles and bells. To his astonishment, the
white mare started forward as if struck and seemed to
shudder under the weight. "Whoa!" She shivered invol-
untarily again. His astonishment and impatience increasing, he put on her bridle, but having buckled it, caressed
her silky nostrils and spoke to her softly. She seemed to
understand. Gently, little by little, he backed her into his
little covered cart bearing his pots and pans, his food, and
the red-and-white striped awnings and poles of his stall.

They joined the long line of brightly painted caravans

and the great engines drawing the roundabouts. The white mare was quiet. She moved steadily, as if the shouting and rattle of departure had awakened her against herself. Lanko walked at her side, relieved but silent, chewing a straw. Now and then, when the mare seemed to hesitate and slacken her pace again, he stroked her side, encouraging her with whispered reminders that they had not far to go. It was autumn and the red of the trees, the heavy dew sparkling on the dying grass, and the frosty smell in the air reminded him how often he and the mare had traveled this way, how she had never failed him, and how always, as on this morning, the jingle of the bells on her bridle had filled him with happiness.

Soon afterward the sun broke out, shedding a soft, sudden light on that long line gleaming like a multicolored snake over the road. It seemed to bring out also not only color but smell, so that besides the scent of frosty leaves and decay, Lanko suddenly caught all the odors that were precious to him: the smell of horses and straw, of cooked herrings, of onions and cabbage, of oil and the smoke belched out far ahead. It seemed difficult to believe he was not young again, so fresh and strong were these smells, as if coming to him for the first time.

Suddenly he was aroused out of these memories by the white mare. Her bells had ceased jingling. She had become perfectly still.

Lanko caressed her head with one hand and patted her side with the other. Again he consoled her, as he consoled himself, with the whisper that they had not far to go. As if understanding this she went on again. With the habit of fifteen years he fell in with her slow, patient, and uncomplaining step.

"Good girl, good girl."

The tinkle of her bells was once more a delight to him. His deep, dark-browed eyes shone. In the sunshine the mare's coat gleamed like silk.

The journey did not seem long to him, but sometimes the mare seemed to lose all courage and would stop again, shivering, staring ahead and breathing hard, so that her sides rose and fell under his hand. Each time by consoling and caressing her he managed to make her go again. Gradually, however, her pauses grew more frequent, her breathing so difficult as to be almost agonizing, and her struggles to draw the cart were terrible.

Lanko dropped behind the rest of the line. Now, however, the thought that he would be crowded out at the pitching did not trouble him. He began to see, even though with intense reluctance, that the mare was not stubborn or capricious, but ill. He began to reproach himself for having kicked her, even for having struck her. His efforts to atone for this were desperately tender, made up of all his softest coaxings, the whispers of his deepest understanding.

"Good girl, good girl! Ain't far now. Steady! Ain't far."

They arrived at last. In the only remaining pitch, in one corner of the ground, he unharnessed the mare. As before she stood very still, uncomplaining, until he had finished. Then suddenly, as if only the burden of the harness and the existence of the cart behind her had borne her up since morning, she sank down into the grass at his feet.

Lanko knelt down too, impelled by astonishment and fear. Her head was still upright but the nostrils were faintly distended and from the mouth hung a little foam, like the slobbering of a child. The look in her eyes, sick and remote, began, even then, to grow deeper. It drove away very slowly but certainly all the intelligence, all the softness and understanding that had gathered there during the years of her life. Comprehending suddenly the gravity of this, Lanko opened her mouth and touched her tongue. Her mouth seemed to him full of the deathly heat of a fever.

He stared at her for a long moment. She seemed to him to grow no worse. It was not yet afternoon, and he began to console himself with the thought that she would be able to rest there all day and all night—even for nearly a week, if need be.

"Good girl, good girl," he whispered to her.

An inspiration seized him. He fetched water in a bucket and held it to her lips in the profound hope that he had found her remedy. As in the morning, at the pool, however, she would not drink. In desperation he cajoled and pleaded with her; she seemed to him to turn away at last with all the weariness and distaste of a deadly sickness.

Afternoon drew on. The painted poles of the stalls and the tops of the great roundabouts began to show themselves against the sky. Lanko unpacked his belongings, then let them remain where they had fallen on the grass. He could not think of trade, and after lighting a fire he boiled up a concoction which it seemed to him, if only he could persuade or force the mare to drink it, must ease her before morning. All the time the mare crouched in the grass, the deathly sickness of her eyes growing steadily more terrible. And though she stared unblinking ahead she seemed oblivious not only of Lanko but of the commotion going on before her and of the trees and the sky, of the whole world itself.

The faith in the remedy he had spent so long in preparing made Lanko approach her at last with both an entreaty and a smile on his lips. "Good girl. Drink. Good girl." He opened her mouth.

When he brought the medicine to her lips, they closed suddenly again. He tried to be patient, to be calm. Again he stroked her soft nostrils and put his head against hers. In this way he told her not to be afraid, that he was only nursing her. But her lips would not remain open. Again and again they closed, feverish and clammy with foam, trembling as if both from fear and sickness. Sweat came out on Lanko's brow; he also trembled.

"Good girl, good girl!" he repeated.

Now she seemed to make no conscious effort to withstand him. It was as if the fever seized and held her mouth closed, until she was rigid and terrified beneath it. She became exhausted quickly, with the result that while she had no power to withstand Lanko she had also none to repulse the tenacity of the sickness.

The medicine grew cold at Lanko's side. For a little while he felt helpless, full only of a dejected wonder that the strong, patient, silky body of the white mare should sink to this. Once again, and now more bitterly, he reproached himself for the blows and the single kick he had given her that morning. That might have begun it, he thought. Suddenly this enraged him, quickened him into life.

He left the mare and, running off, seized the first man he knew. It was the Fat Lady man, the one with whom he had begun the argument so trivial and ridiculous that neither could remember on what subject it had been. Lanko seized him.

"Come and look at my old mare a minute!"

They went and knelt at the mare's side. She seemed to have sickened, even in those few moments, more rapidly and terribly than ever before.

"Look at her, look at her!"

The other spent a long time regarding her. Unable at last to bear this any longer, Lanko said, "What is it? What do you think it is?"

Before them the mare grew visibly weaker, breathing with pathetic effort. The Fat Lady man answered in low tones, "You don't know. It might be anything."

Lanko began to talk with intense desperation, explaining it all. "I couldn't get her to drink this morning, not anyhow. Then on the road she kept lagging and stopping." His voice fell a little. "After that, just as we got here, she fell down and hasn't been up since. She can't get up."

The Fat Lady man indicated the medicine and said slowly, "We'll try her with that again. See if that'll do anything."

Lanko heated the concoction again and brought it to the white mare's lips. He had become more than ever patient, fuller of sympathy and care.

"Open her mouth—gently," he asked. The Fat Lady man was tender also. Very slowly he forced open the lips, which, having no longer the power to hold their own spittle, let it run down his wrists and arms in a pitiful, deathly flow. To his attentions there came no resistance, no struggle. Into the mouth held open thus, without strength or spirit, Lanko poured some of the medicine.

Along the mare's neck ran a ripple or two; he poured in a little more, making more ripples in her silky flesh, and so on until she had drunk it all. The Fat Lady man let the lips close again. "Good girl, good girl," Lanko whispered.

Both men rose to their feet. "You can't do no more than that," the Fat Lady man whispered. "Let her be. Keep her still. Put something over her."

"What is it? What do you think it is?"

"You don't know. It might be anything."

He went off, and over the mare Lanko laid sacks and a blanket or two. Again he told himself he must be patient and calm. So long as she kept up her head, even though with the sickness staring from her eyes, there was hope. This thought began to obsess him. It caused him to turn sharply at intervals, wherever he was, and gaze at her. Without exception her head remained where it had been ever since she had fallen. "Good girl, good girl," he whispered.

Dusk began to fall; a cool mist formed mysteriously over the grass. In the fair itself lights sprang up from the vans; here and there was a paraffin flare. Lanko found consolation even in these things. Tonight at least, since the fair was not yet open, there would be no noise, no organs, no shrieks, no commotion.

The covered flanks of the mare lay motionless, uncomplaining, expressive of her quiet and stoical spirit. To his joy her head did not droop again. At her side he sat and watched, looking at her as if to say, "Tell me what I can do! Good girl, good girl."

Out of the surrounding darkness began to come figures. One by one they bent and looked at the mare as she half

lay, half sat in the grass, and then to Lanko expressed
their opinions. He knew them all; he recognized the voices
of the men who had jeered good-naturedly at him that
morning by the drinking pool. Their dark, check-shirted,
red-shirted, swarthy figures blacked out the light of his
fire. He saw the coconut man, the Aunt Sallys, the shooting men, the skittleboard and bagatelle owners, the watch-
and-clock men with rings on their fat fingers, the joy-
wheel proprietor, the peacock man, his wife with long
rings in her ears. The Fat Lady herself came too. Each of
them looked at the white mare, some even touched her,
all of them spoke to Lanko kindly, answering his per-
sistent and desperate little inquiries with tact, with bluff,
in whatever manner seemed to them best for keeping alive
his hope in her ebbing life.

In each of them he found something for which to be
thankful. He discovered too that his spirits did not droop,
that he had now such faith in the mare as never before.
It even seemed to him that, so far from drooping, her
head had raised itself a little. In the darkness, also, the
sickness seemed to have been driven from her eyes.

The men continued their advice, their calm bluff, the
sympathies of their understanding yet undeceived minds.
"You can't tell—know better in the morning—might be
over in a week or a day." They spoke with the difficult
care of men seeking to conceal a painful truth. Then one
by one they wandered off slowly, as if reluctantly, into
the darkness.

Lanko and the white mare were alone again. Her head
had drooped, her flanks were steadier, she seemed at rest,
he thought. He fell into reminiscences about her, of her

early days, when she too had cantered, had borne her head with an arched, beautifully shadowed neck, when he had had to cut her tail in order to keep it from dragging on the ground. In those days he had not only decorated her with bells, but with colored ribbons and cords and painted banners. She had traveled everywhere with him, in springtime, in summer and autumn, and in winter had camped with him or had been stabled in some village while he traded. In his mind he could see her anywhere— on the road, in the meadows, at the fairs—with her white reflection in the drinking pools where they went.

Suddenly he looked up. It was very dark, his fire became momentarily dim, but he saw that her head had fallen. Very slowly he crawled on his hands and knees toward her. He saw that what he had for so long dreaded and hoped against had taken place and was still going on. He could see, even as he came up to her, that her head was lowering in fast, spasmodic jerks, her mane falling across her black eyes, the sickly foam once again dripping from her lips. He leaned forward and took her head in his hands, striving to hold it erect in spite of its heaviness, smoothing back her mane as he might have done a child's hair. He wiped the foam from her lips with the sleeve of his coat. He spoke to her. Here he knew was the test of his patience, of his fidelity. He exerted his strength in order to keep her head from sinking a fraction. "Good girl, good girl," he whispered.

Suddenly she sank beyond his grasp. As if unable to realize the swiftness of it all, he raised her head again and held it in his arms. She was still warm. She raised a murmur. This sound, either of protest or pain, seemed to strike him like something cold, in the center of his breast. It crept to his heart. Her head sank to the ground. There was silence. He could not even call to her.

But into her soft, silky flanks, still warm for him with the memory of a life so recently there, he suddenly buried his face. His lips opened as if to say something, but nothing came, and they closed without a sound.

On the dark grass, as if understanding, the white mare lay silent too.

JEREMY RODOCK
Jack Schaefer

Jeremy Rodock was a hanging man when it came to horse thieves. He hanged them quick and efficient, and told what law there was about it afterward. He was a big man in many ways and not just in shadow-making size. People knew him. He had a big ranch—a horse ranch—about the biggest in the Territory, and he loved horses, and no one, not even one of his own hands—and they were carefully picked—could match him at breaking and gentling his big geldings for any kind of roadwork. Tall they were, those horses, and rawboned, out of Western mares by some hackney stallions he'd had brought from the East, and after you'd been working with cow ponies they'd set

149

you back on your heels when you first saw them. But they were stout in harness with a fast, swinging trot that could take the miles and a heavy coach better than anything else on hoofs. He was proud of those horses, and he had a right to be. I know. I was one of his hands for a time. I was with him once when he hanged a pair of rustlers. And I was with him the one time he didn't.

That was a long ways back. I was young then with a stretch in my legs, about topping twenty, and Jeremy Rodock was already an old man. Maybe not so old, maybe just about into his fifties, but he seemed old to me—old the way a pine gets when it's through growing, standing tall and straight and spreading strong, but with the graying grimness around the edges that shows it's settling to the long last stand against the winds and the storms. I remember I was surprised he could still outwork any of his men and be up before them in the morning. He was tough fiber clear through, and he took me on because I had a feeling for horses and they'd handle for me without much fuss, and that was what he wanted. "You'll earn your pay," he said, "and not act your age more than you can help, and if your sap breaks out in sass, I'll slap you against a gatepost and larrup the hide off your back." And he would, and I knew it. And he taught me plenty about horses and men, and I worked for him the way I've never worked for another man.

That was the kind of work I liked. We always paired for it, and Rodock was letting me side him. The same men, working as a team, always handled the same horses from the time they were brought in off the range until the time they were ready and delivered. They were plenty wild at first, four- and five-year-olds with free roaming strong in their legs, not having had any experience with men and ropes from the time they were foaled except for the few days they were halterbroken and bangtailed as coming two-year-olds. They had their growth and life was running in them, and it was a pleasure working with them.

Rodock's system was quick and thorough; you could tell a Rodock horse by the way he'd stand when you wanted him to stand and give all he had when you wanted him to move, and respond to the reins like he knew what you wanted almost before you were certain yourself. We didn't do much with saddle stock except as needed for our personal use. Rodock horses were stage horses. That's what they were bred and broke for. They were all right for riding, maybe better than all right if you could stick their paces, because they sure could cover ground, but they were best for stage work.

We'd rope a horse out of the corral and take him into a square stall and tie a hind leg up to his belly so he couldn't even try to kick without falling flat, and then start to get acquainted. We'd talk to him until he was used to voices, and slap him and push him around till he knew we weren't going to hurt him. Then we'd throw old harness on him and yank it off and throw it on again, and keep at this till he'd stand without flicking an inch of hide no matter how hard the harness hit. We'd take him out and let the leg down and lead him around with the old harness flapping till that wouldn't mean any more to him than a breeze blowing. We'd fit him with reins, and one man would walk in front with the lead rope and

the other behind holding the reins and ease him into
knowing what they meant. And all the time we'd speak
sharp when he acted up and speak soft and give him a
piece of carrot or a fistful of corn when he behaved right.

Hitching was a different proposition. No horse that'll
work for you because he wants to, and not just because
he's beat into it, takes kindly to hitching. He's bound to
throw his weight about the first time or two and seem
to forget a lot he's learned. We'd take our horse and
match him with a well-broke trainer, and harness the
two of them with good leather to a stout wagon. We'd
have half hobbles on his front feet fastened to the spliced
ends of a rope that ran up through a ring on the under-
side of his girth and through another ring on a wagon
tongue and up to the driving seat. Then the two of us
would get on the seat and I'd hold the rope and Rodock
would take the reins. The moment we'd start to move, the
trainer heaving into the traces, things would begin to
happen. The new horse would be mighty surprised. He'd
likely start rearing or plunging. I'd pull on the rope and
his front legs would come out from under him and down
he'd go on his nose.

After trying that a few times, he'd learn he wasn't
getting anywhere and begin to steady and remember some
of the things he'd learned before. He'd find he had to
step along when the wagon moved, and after a while
he'd find that stepping was smoothest and easiest if he
did his share of the pulling. Whenever he'd misbehave
or wouldn't stop when he should, I'd yank on the rope
and his nose would hit the soft dirt. It was surprising how
quick he'd learn to put his weight into the harness and
pay attention to the boss riding behind him. Sometimes,

in a matter of three weeks, we'd have one ready to take his place in a four-horse pull of the old coach we had for practice runs. That would be a good horse.

Well, we were readying twenty-some teams for a new stage line when this happened. Maybe it wouldn't have happened, not the way it did, if one of the horses hadn't sprung a tendon and we needed a replacement. I don't blame myself for it, and I don't think Rodock did either, even though the leg went bad when I pulled the horse down on his nose. He was something of a hollow head anyway, and wasn't learning as he should and had kept on trying to smash loose every time the wagon moved.

As I say, this horse pulled a tendon, not bad, but enough to mean a limp, and Rodock wouldn't send a limping horse along even to a man he might otherwise be willing to trim on a close deal. Shoo him out on the range, he told me, and let time and rest and our good grass put him in shape for another try next year. "And saddle my bay," he said, "and take any horse you'd care to sit, Son. We'll ramble out to the lower basin and bring in another and maybe a spare in case something else happens."

That was why we were riding out a little before noon on a hot day, leaving the others busy about the buildings, just the two of us loafing along toward the first of the series of small natural valleys on Rodock's range where he kept the geldings and young studs. We were almost there, riding the ridge, when he stopped and swung in the saddle toward me. "Let's make a day of it, Son. Let's mosey on to the next basin and have a look-see at the mares there and this year's crop of foals. I like to see the little critters run."

That's what I mean. If we hadn't been out already, he

never would have taken time to go there. We'd checked the mares a few weeks before and tallied the foals and seen that everything was all right. If that horse hadn't gone lame, it might have been weeks, maybe months, before any of us would have gone that way again.

We moseyed on, not pushing our horses because we'd be using them hard on the way back, cutting out a couple of geldings and hustling them home. We came over the last rise and looked down into that second small valley, and there wasn't a single thing in sight. Where there ought to have been better than forty mares and their foals, there wasn't a moving object, only the grass shading to deeper green down the slope to the trees along the stream and fading out again up the other side of the valley.

Jeremy Rodock sat still in his saddle. "I didn't think anyone would have the nerve," he said, quiet and slow. He put his horse into a trot around the edge of the valley, leaning over and looking at the ground, and I followed. He stopped at the head of the valley, where it narrowed and the stream came through, and he dismounted and went over the ground carefully. He came back to his horse and leaned his chest against the saddle, looking over it and up at me.

"Here's where they were driven out," he said, still quiet and slow. "At least three men. Their horses were shod. Not more than a few days ago. A couple of weeks and there wouldn't be any trail left to follow." He looked over his saddle and studied me. "You've been with me long enough, Son," he said, "for me to know what you do with horses. But I don't know what you can do with that gun you're carrying. I wish I'd brought one of the older

men. You better head back and give the word. I'm following this trail."

"Mister Rodock," I said, "I wish you wouldn't make
so many remarks about my age. One thing a man can't
help is his age. But anywhere you and that bay can go,
me and this roan can follow. And as for this gun I'm
carrying, I can hit anything with it you can and maybe a
few things you'd miss."

He looked at me over his saddle, and his eyebrows
twitched a little upward. "Careful, Son," he said. "That
comes close to being sass." His jawline tightened, and
he had that old-pine look, gray and grim and enduring.
"You'll have hard riding," he said, and swung into his
saddle and put his horse into a steady trot along the trail,
and that was all he said for the next four-five hours.

Hard riding it was. Trotting gets to a man even if he's
used to being on a horse. It's a jolting pace, and after a
time your muscles grow plain tired of easing the jolts,
and the calluses on your rump warm up and remind you
they're there. But trotting is the way to make time if you
really intend to travel. Some people think the best way is
to keep to a steady lope. That works on the back of your
neck after a while and takes too much out of the horse
after the first couple of hours. Others like to run the
horse, then give him a breather, then run him again, and
keep that up. You take it all out of him the first day doing
that. Trotting is the best way. A good horse can trot along
steady, his shoulders and legs relaxed and his hoofs slapping down almost by their own weight, do it hour after
hour and cover his fifty to sixty miles with no more than
a nice even sweat and be ready to do the same the next

day and the next after that, and a lot longer than any man riding him can hope to take it.

Rodock was trotting, and his long-legged bay was swinging out the miles, and far as I could tell the old man was made of iron and didn't even know he was taking a beating. I knew I was, and that roan I'd picked because he looked like a cow pony I'd had once, was working with his shorter legs to hold the pace, and I was shifting my weight from one side to the other about every fifteen minutes so I'd burn only half of my rump at a time.

It was dark night when Rodock stopped by water and swung down and hobbled his horse and unsaddled, and I did the same. "Might miss the trail in the dark," he said. "Anyways, they're moving slow on account of the colts. I figure we've gained at least a day on them already. Maybe more. Better get some sleep. We'll be traveling with the first light." He settled down with his saddle for a pillow and I did the same, and after a few minutes his voice drifted out of the darkness. "You came along right well, Son. Do the same tomorrow, and I'll shut up about your age."

Next thing I knew he was shaking me awake and the advance glow of the sun was climbing the sky, and he was squatting beside me with a hatful of berries from the bushes near the water. I ate my share and we saddled and started on, and after I shook the stiffness I felt fresh and almost chipper. The trail was snaking in wide curves southwest, following the low places, but rising, as the whole country was, gradually up through the foothills toward the first tier of mountains.

About regular breakfast time, when the sun was a couple of hours over the horizon behind us, Rodock waved to me to come alongside close. "None of this makes sense," he said, without slacking pace. "A queer kind of rustling runoff. Mares and foals. I've tangled with a lot of thievery in my time, but all of it was with stock could be moved fast and disposed of quick. Can't do that with mares and sucking colts. How do you figure it, Son?"

I studied that awhile. "Mister Rodock," I said, "there's only one advantage I see. Colts that young haven't felt a branding iron yet. Get away with them, and you can slap on any brand you want."

"You're aging fast, Son," he said. "That's a right good thought. But these foals couldn't be weaned for three months yet. Say two months if you were the kind could be mean and not worry about getting them started right. What good would they be, even with your brand on them, still nursing mares that have got my J-tailed-R brand."

"I'd be mighty embarrassed," I said, "every time anybody had a look at a one of them. Guess I'd have to keep them out of sight till they could be weaned."

"For two-three months, Son?" he said. "You'd ride herd on them two-three months to keep them from heading back to their home range? Or coop them someplace where you'd have to feed them? And be worrying all the time that maybe Jeremy Rodock would jump you with a hanging rope in his hand?"

"No," I said. "I wouldn't. I don't know what I'd do. Guess I just don't have a thieving mind."

"But somebody's doing it," he said. "Damn if I know what."

And we moved along at that steady fast trot, and my roan dropped back where he'd liked to stay, about twenty feet behind where he could set his own rhythm without being bothered trying to match the strides of the longer-legged bay. We moved along, and I began to feel empty clear down into my shanks and I began to hunch forward to ease the calluses on my rump. The only break all morning was a short stop for brief watering. We moved along and into the afternoon, and I could tell the roan felt exactly as I did. He and I were concentrating on just one thing, putting all we had into following twenty feet after an old iron ramrod of a man on one of the long-legged, tireless horses of his own shrewd breeding.

The trail was still stale, several days at least, and we were not watching sharp ahead, so we came on them suddenly. Rodock, being ahead and going up a rise, saw them first and was swinging to the ground and grabbing his horse's nose when I came beside him and saw the herd, bunched, well ahead and into a small canyon that cut off to the right. I swung down and caught the roan's nose in time to stop the nicker starting, and we hurried to lead both horses back down the rise and a good ways more and over to a clump of trees. We tied them there and went ahead again on foot, crawling the last stretch up the rise and dropping on our bellies to peer over the top. They were there all right, the whole herd, the mares grazing quietly, some of the foals lying down, the others skittering around the way they do, daring each other to flip their heels.

We studied that scene a long time, checking every square yard of it as far as we could see. There was not a man or a saddled horse in sight. Rodock plucked a blade of grass and stuck it in his mouth and chewed on it.

"All right, Son," he said. "Seems we'll have to smoke them out. They must be holed up somewhere handy waiting to see if anyone's following. You scout around the left side of that canyon, and I'll take the right. Watch for tracks and keep an eye cocked behind you. We'll meet way up there beyond the herd where the trees and bushes give good cover. If you're jumped, get off a shot and I'll be on my way over a-humping."

"Mister Rodock," I said, "you do the same and so will I."

We separated, slipping off our different ways and moving slow behind any cover that showed. I went along the left rim of the canyon, crouching by rocks and checking the ground carefully each time before moving on and peering down into the canyon along the way. I came on a snake and circled it and flushed a rabbit out of some bushes, and those were the only living things or signs of them I saw except for the horses below there in the canyon. Well up beyond them, where the rock wall slanted out into a passable slope, I worked my way down and to where we were to meet. I waited, and after a while Rodock appeared, walking toward me without even trying to stay under cover.

"See anything, Son?" he said.

"No," I said.

"It's crazier than ever," he said. "I found their tracks where they left. Three shod horses moving straight out. Now what made them chuck and run like that? Tracks at least a day old too."

"Somebody scared them," I said.

"It would take a lot," he said, "to scare men with nerve enough to make off with a bunch of my horses. Who'd be roaming around up here anyway? If it was anyone living within a hundred miles, they'd know my brand and be taking the horses in." He stood there straight, hands on his hips, and stared down the canyon at the herd. "What's holding them?" he said.

"Holding who?" I said.

"Those horses," he said. "Those mares. Why haven't they headed for home? Why aren't they working along as they graze?"

He was right. They weren't acting natural. They were bunched too close and hardly moving, and when any of them did move there was something wrong. We stared at them, and suddenly Rodock began to run toward them and I had trouble staying close behind him. They heard us and turned to face us and they had trouble turning, and Rodock stopped and stared at them and there was a funny moaning sound in his throat.

"My God!" he said. "Look at their front feet!"

I looked, and I could see right away what he meant. They had been roped and thrown and their front hoofs rasped almost to the quick, so that they could barely put their weight on them. Each step hurt, and they couldn't have traveled at all off the canyon grass out on the rocky ground beyond. It hurt me seeing them hurt each time they tried to move, and if it did that to me I could imagine what it did to Jeremy Rodock.

They knew him, and some of them nickered at him, and the old mare that was their leader, and was standing with head drooping, raised her head and started forward and dropped her head again and limped to us with it hanging almost to the ground. There was a heavy iron bolt tied to her forelock and hanging down between her eyes. You know how a horse moves its head as it walks. This bolt would have bobbed against her forehead with each step she took, and already it had broken through the skin and worn a big sore that was beginning to fester.

Rodock stood still and stared at her, and that moaning sound clung in his throat. I had to do something. I pulled out my pocketknife and cut through the tied hairs and tossed the bolt far as I could. I kicked up a piece of sod and reached down and took a handful of clean dirt and rubbed it over the sore on her forehead and then wiped it and the oozing stuff away with my neckerchief, and she stood for me and only shivered as I rubbed. I looked at Rodock, and he was someone I had never seen before. He was a gaunt figure of a man, with eyes pulled back deep in their sockets and burning, and the bones of his face showing plain under the flesh.

"Mister Rodock," I said, "are we riding out on that three-horse trail?" I don't think he even heard me.

"Not a thing," he said. "Not a single solitary god-damned thing I can do. They're traveling light and fast now. Too much of a start and too far up in the rocks for trailing. They've probably separated and could be head-ing clean out of the Territory. They're devilish smart and they've done it, and there's not a goddamned thing I can do."

"We've got the mares," I said. "And the foals."

He noticed me, a flick of his eyes at me. "We've got them way up here, and they can't be moved. Not until those hoofs grow out." He turned toward me and threw words at me, and I wasn't anyone he knew, just someone to be a target for his bitterness. "They're devils! Three devils! Nothing worth the name of man would treat horses like that. See the devilishness of it? They run my horses way up here and cripple them. They don't have to stay around. The horses can't get away. They knew the chances are we won't miss the mares for weeks, and by then the trail will be overgrown and we won't know which way they went and waste time combing the whole damn country in every direction, and maybe never get up in here. Even if someone follows them soon, like we did, they're gone and can't be caught. One of them can slip back every week or two to see what's going, and if he's nabbed, what can tie him to the runoff? He's just a fiddle foot riding through. By weaning time, if nothing has happened, they can hurry in and take the colts and get off clean with a lot of unbranded horseflesh. And there's not a thing we can do."

"We can watch the mares," I said, "till they're able to travel some, then push them home by easy stages. And meantime be mighty rough on anyone comes noseying around."

"We've got the mares," he said. "They're as well off here as anywhere now. What I want is those devils. All three of them. Together and roped and in my hands." He put out his hands, the fingers clawed, and shook them at me. "I've got to get them! Do you see that? I've got to!" He dropped his hands limp at his sides, and his voice dropped too, dry and quiet with a coldness in it. "There's one thing we can do. We can leave everything as it is and go home and keep our mouths shut and wait and be here when they come for the colts." He took me by the shoulders, and his fingers hurt my muscles. "You see what they did to my horses. Can you keep your mouth shut?"

He didn't wait for me to answer. He let go of my shoulders and turned and went straight through the herd

of crippled mares without looking at them and on down
the canyon and out and over the rise where we first sighted
them and on to the clump of trees where we had tied our
horses.

I followed him and he was mounted and already starting off when I reached the roan, and I mounted and set
out after him. He was in no hurry now and let the bay
walk part of the time, and the roan and I were glad of
that. He never turned to look at me or seemed to notice
whether I followed or not. A rabbit jumped out of the
brush, and I knocked it over on the second shot, and
picked it up and laid it on the saddle in front of me, and
he paid no attention to me, not even to the shots, just
steadying the bay when it started at the sharp sounds and
holding it firm on the back trail.

He stopped by a stream while there was still light and
dismounted, and I did the same. After we had hobbled
and unsaddled the horses, he sat on the ground with his
back to a rock and stared into space. I couldn't think of
anything to say, so I gathered some wood and made a fire.
I took my knife and gutted the rabbit and cut off the
head. I found some fairly good clay and moistened it and
rolled the rabbit in a ball of it and dropped this in the
fire. When I thought it would be about done, I poked it
out of the hot ashes and let it cool a bit. Then I pried off
the baked clay and the skin came with it and the meat
showed juicy and smelled fine. It was still a little raw, but
anything would have tasted good then. I passed Rodock
some pieces, and he took them and ate the meat off the
bones mechanically like his mind was far away someplace.
I still couldn't think of anything to say, so I stretched out
with my head on my saddle, and then it was morning and

I was chilled and stiff and staring up at clear sky, and he was coming toward me leading both horses and his already saddled.

It was getting toward noon, and we were edging onto our home range when we met two of the regular hands out looking for us. They came galloping with a lot of questions, and Rodock put up a palm to stop them.

"Nothing's wrong," he said. "I took a sudden mind to circle around and look over some of the stock that's strayed a bit and show the boy here parts of my range he hadn't seen before. Went further'n I intended to and we're some tuckered. You two cut over to the lower basin and take in a pair of four-year-olds. Hightail it straight and don't dawdle. We've got that stage order to meet."

They were maybe a mite puzzled as they rode off, but it was plain they hadn't hit the second basin and seen the mares were missing. Rodock and I started on, and I thought of something to say and urged the roan close.

"Mister Rodock," I said, "I don't like that word *boy.*"

"That's too bad," he said, and went steadily on and I followed, and he paid no more attention to me all the rest of the way to the ranch buildings.

Things were different after that around the place. He didn't work with the horses himself anymore. Most of the time he stayed in his sturdy frame house where he had a Mexican to cook for him and fight the summer dust, and I don't know what he did in there. Once in a while he'd be on the porch, and he'd sit there hours staring off where the foothills started their climb toward the mountains. With him shut away like that, I was paired with Hugh Claggett. This Claggett was a good enough man, I guess. Rodock thought some of him. They had knocked around together years back, and then he had showed up needing a job sometime before I was around the place. Rodock gave him one, and he was a sort of acting foreman when Rodock was away for any reason. He knew horses, maybe as much as Rodock himself in terms of the things you could put down as fact in a book. But he didn't have the real feel, the deep inside feel, of them that means you can sense what's going on inside a horse's head; walk up to a rolled-eye maverick that's pawing the sky at the end of a rope the way Rodock could, and talk the non-sense out of him and have him standing there quivering to quiet under your hand in a matter of minutes. Claggett was a precise, practical sort of a man, and working with him was just that, working, and I took no real pleasure in it.

When Rodock did come down by the stables and work-ing corral, he was different. He didn't come often, and it would have been better if he hadn't come at all. First thing I noticed was his walk. There was no bounce to it. Always before, no matter how tired he was, he walked rolling on the soles of his feet from heels to toes and coming off the toes each step with a little bouncy spring. Now he was walking flatfooted, plodding, like he was carrying more weight than just his body. And he was hard and driving in a new way, a nasty and irritable way. He'd always been one to find fault, but that had been because he was better at his business than any of us and he wanted to set us straight. He'd shrivel us down to size with a good clean tongue whipping, then pitched in himself and show us how to do whatever it was and we'd be the better for it.

Now he was plain cussed all through. He'd snap at us

about anything and everything. Nothing we did was right. He'd not do a lick of work himself, just stand by and find fault, and his voice was brittle and nasty, and he'd get personal in his remarks. And he was mighty touchy about how we treated the horses. We did the way he had taught us and the way I knew was right by how the horses handled. Still, he would blow red and mad and tear into us with bitter words saying we were slapping on leather too hard or fitting bridles too snug, little things, but they added to a nagging tally as the days passed and made our work tiring and troublesome. There was a lot of grumbling going on in the bunkhouse in the evenings.

Time and again I wanted to tell the others about the mares so maybe they'd understand. But I'd remember his hands stretching toward me and shaking and then biting into my shoulders, and then I'd keep what had happened blocked inside me. I knew what was festering in him. I'd wake at night thinking about those mares, thinking about them way up there in the hills pegged to a small space of thinning grass by hoofs that hurt when weight came on them and sent stabs of pain up their legs when they hit anything hard.

A good horse is a fine-looking animal. But it isn't the appearance that gets into you and makes something in you reach out and respond to him. It's the way he moves, the sense of movement in him even when he's standing still, the clean-stepping speed and competence of him that's born in him and is what he is and is his reason for being. Take that away and he's a pitiful thing. And somewhere there were three men who had done that to those mares. I'd jump awake at night and think about them and maybe have some notion of what it cost Jeremy

Rodock to stay set there at his ranch and leave his mares alone with their misery far off up in the hills.

When the stage horses were ready to be shod for the last real road tests, he nearly drove our blacksmith crazy cursing every time a hoof was trimmed or one of them flinched under the hammer. We finished them off with hard runs in squads hitched to the old coach and delivered them, and then there was nothing much to do. Not another order was waiting. Several times agents had been to see Rodock and had gone into the house and come out again and departed, looking downright peeved. I don't know whether he simply refused any more orders or acted so mean that they wouldn't do business with him.

Anyway, it was bad all around. There was too much loafing time. Except for a small crew making hay close in, no one was sent out on the range at all. The men were dissatisfied and they had reason to be, and they took to quarreling with each other. Some of them quit in disgust and others after arguing words with Rodock, and finally the last bunch demanded their time together and left, and Claggett and I were the only ones still there. That's not counting the Mexican, but he was housebroke and not worth counting. Claggett and I could handle the chores for the few horses kept regularly around the place and still have time to waste. We played euchre, but I never could beat him and then got tired of trying. And Rodock sat on his porch and stared into the distance. I didn't think he even noticed me when I figured that his bay would be getting soft and started saddling him and taking him out for exercise the same as I did the roan.

One day I rode him right past the porch. Rodock fooled

me on that, though. I was almost past, pretending not to see him, when his voice flicked at me. "Easy on those reins, boy. They're just extra trimming. That horse knows what you want by the feel of your legs around him. I don't want him spoiled." He was right too. I found you could put that bay through a figure eight or drop him between two close-set posts just by thinking it down through your legs.

The slow days went by, and I couldn't stand it any longer. I went to the house. "Mister Rodock," I said, "it's near two months now. Isn't it time we made a move?"

"Don't be so damn young," he said. "I'll move when I know it's right."

I stood on one foot and then on the other, and I couldn't think of anything to say except what I'd said before about my age, so I went back to the bunkhouse and made Claggett teach me all the games of solitaire he knew.

Then one morning I was oiling harness to keep it limber when I looked up and Rodock was in the stable doorway.

"Saddle my bay," he said, "and Hugh's sorrel. I reckon that roan'll do for you again. Pick out a good packhorse and bring them all around to the storehouse soon as you can."

I jumped to do what he said, and when I had the horses there he and Claggett had packs filled. We loaded the extra horse, and the last thing Rodock did was hand out Henrys, and we tucked these in our saddle scabbards and started out. He led the way, and from the direction he took it was plain we were not heading straight into the hills, but were going to swing around and come in from the south.

I led the packhorse and we rode in a compact bunch, not pushing for speed. It was in the afternoon that we ran into the other riders, out from the settlement and heading our way: Ben Kern, who was Federal Marshal for that part of the Territory, and three of the men he usually swore in as deputies when he had a need for any. We stopped and they stopped, looking us over.

"You've saved me some miles," Kern said. "I was heading for your place."

Rodock raised his eyebrows and looked at him and was silent. I kept my mouth shut. Claggett, who probably knew as much about the mares as I did by now, did the same. This was Rodock's game.

"Not saying much, are you?" Kern said. He saw the Henrys. "Got your war paint on, too. I thought something would be doing from what I've been hearing about things at your place. What's on your mind this time?"

"My mind's my own," Rodock said. "But it could be we're off on a little camping trip."

"And again it couldn't," Kern said. "Only camping you ever do is on the tail of a horse thief. That's the trouble. Twice now you've written in to tell me where to find them swinging. Evidence was clear enough, so there wasn't much I could do. But you're too damn free with your rope. How we going to get decent law around here with you old-timers crossing things up? This time, if it is a this time, you're doing it right and turn them over to me. We'll just ride along to see that you do it."

Rodock turned to me. He had that grim and enduring look, and the lines by his mouth were taut. "Break out those packs, boy. We're camping right here." I saw what he was figuring, and I dismounted and began unfastening the packs. I had them on the ground and was fussing with the knots when Kern spoke.

"You're a stubborn old bastard," he said. "You'd stay right here and outwait us."

"I would," Rodock said.

"All right," Kern said. "We'll fade. But I've warned you. If it's rustlers you're after, bring them to me."

Rodock didn't say a thing and I heaved the packs on the horse again and by the time I had them fastened tight, Kern and his men were a distance away and throwing dust. We started on, and by dark we had gone a good piece. By dark the next day we had made a big half circle and were well into the hills. About noon of the next, we were close enough to the canyon where we had found the mares, say two miles if you could have hopped it straight. Claggett and I waited while Rodock scouted around. He came back and led us up a twisting rocky draw to a small parkway by a fifteen-foot rock shelf and the rest of the way by a close stand of pine. It was about a half acre in size, and you'd never know it was there unless you came along the draw and stumbled into it.

We picketed the horses there and headed for the canyon on foot, moving slow and cautious as we came close. When we peered over the rim, the herd was there all right, the foals beginning to get some growth and the mares stepping a lot easier than before. They were used to the place now and not interested in leaving. They had taken to ranging pretty far up the canyon, but we managed to sight the whole count after a few minutes' watching.

We searched along the rim for the right spot and found it, a crack in the rim wide enough for a man to ease into comfortably and be off the skyline for anyone looking from below, yet able to see the whole stretch where the herd was. To make it even better, we hauled a few rocks to the edge of the opening and piled brush with them, leaving a careful spyhole. We brought a flat-topped rock for a seat behind the hole. The idea was that one of us could sit there watching while the other two holed in a natural hiding place some fifty feet back under an over-hanging ledge with a good screen of brush. The signal, if anything happened, was to be a pebble chucked back toward the hiding place.

I thought we'd take turns watching, but Rodock settled on that flat-top stone and froze there. Claggett and I kept each other company under the ledge, if you could call it keeping company when one person spent most of the time with his mouth shut whittling endless shavings off chunks of old wood or taking naps. That man Claggett had no nerves. He could keep his knife going for an hour at a time without missing a stroke or stretch out and drop off into a nap like we were just lazing around at the ranch. He didn't seem to have much personal interest in what might develop. He was just doing a job and tagging along with an old-time partner. As I said before, he didn't have a real feel for horses. I guess to be fair to him I ought to remember that he hadn't seen those mares with their hoofs rasped to the quick and flinching and shuddering with every step they took.

Me, I was strung like a too-tight fiddle. I'd have cracked sure if I hadn't had the sense to bring a deck in my pocket for solitaire. I nearly wore out those cards and even took to cheating to win, and it seemed to me we were cooped there for weeks when it was only five days. And all the

time, every day, Rodock sat on that stone as if he was a
piece of it, getting older and grayer and grimmer.

Nights we spent back with the horses. We'd be moving
before dawn each morning, eating a heavy breakfast
cooked over a small quick fire, then slipping out to our
places with the first streaks of light carrying a cold snack
in our pockets. We'd return after dark for another quick
meal and roll right afterward into our blankets. You'd
think we hardly knew each other the way we behaved,
only speaking when that was necessary. Claggett was
never much of a talker, and Rodock was tied so tight in
himself now he didn't have a word to spare. I kept quiet
because I didn't want him smacking my age at me again.
If he could chew his lips and wear out the hours waiting,
I could too, and I did.

We were well into the fifth day and I was about con-
vinced nothing would ever happen again, anytime ever
anywhere in the whole wide world, when a pebble came
snicking through the brush and Rodock came hard after it,
ducking low and hurrying.

"They're here," he said. "All three." And I noticed the
fierce little specks of light beginning to burn in his eyes.
"They're stringing ropes to trees for a corral. Probably
planning to brand here, then run." He looked at me and
I could see him assessing me and dismissing me, and he
turned to Claggett. "Hugh," he started to say, "I want
you to—"

I guess it was the way he had looked at me and the
things he had said about my age. Anyway, I was mad. I
didn't know what he was going to say, but I knew he had
passed me by. I grabbed him by the arm. "Mister Rodock,"
I said, "I'm the one rode with you after those mares."

He stared at me and shook his head a little as if to clear it. "All right, boy," he said. "You do this and by God you do it right. Hurry back and get your horse and swing around and come riding into the canyon. Far as I can tell at the distance, these men are strangers, so there's not much chance they'd know you worked for me. You're just a drifter riding through. Keep them talking, so Hugh and I can get down behind them. If they start something, keep them occupied long as you can." He grabbed me by the shoulders the way he had when we found the mares. "Any shooting you do, shoot to miss. I want them alive." He let go of me. "Now scat."

I scatted. I never went so fast over rough country on my own feet in my life. When I reached the roan, I had to hang onto his neck to get some breath and my strength back. I slapped my saddle on and took him a good clip out of the draw and in a sharp circle for the canyon mouth, a good clip, but not too much to put him in a lather. I was heading into the canyon, pulling him to an easy trot, when it hit me, what a damn fool thing I was doing. There were three of them in there, three mighty smart men with a lot of nerve, and they had put a lot of time and waiting into this job and wouldn't likely be wanting to take chances on its going wrong. I was scared, so scared I could hardly sit the roan, and I came near swinging him around and putting my heels to him. Maybe I would have. Maybe I would have run out on those mares. But then I saw that one of the men had spotted me, and there was nothing much to do but keep going toward them.

The one that had spotted me was out a ways from the others as a lookout. He had a rifle and he swung it to cover me as I came near, and I stopped the roan. He was a hardcase specimen if ever I saw one, and I didn't like the way he looked at me.

"Hold it now, Sonny," he said. "Throw down your guns."

I was glad he said that, said "Sonny," I mean, because it sort of stiffened me and I wasn't quite so scared, being taken up some with being mad. I tried to act surprised and hold my voice easy.

"Lookahere," I said, "that's an unfriendly way to talk to a stranger riding through. I wouldn't think of using these guns unless somebody pushed me into it, but I'd feel kind of naked without them. Let's just leave them alone, and if you're not the boss, suppose you let me talk to him that is."

I figured he wouldn't shoot because they'd want to know was I alone and what was I doing around there, and I was right. He jerked his head toward the other two.

"Move along, Sonny," he said. "But slow. And keep your hands high in sight. I'll blast you out of that saddle if you wiggle a finger."

I walked the roan close to the other two and he followed behind me and circled around me to stand with them. They had been starting a fire and had stopped to stare at me coming. One was a short, stocky man, almost bald, with a fringe of grizzled beard down his cheeks and around his chin. The other was about medium height and slender, with clean chiseled features and a pair of the hardest, shrewdest, bluest eyes I ever saw. It was plain he was the boss by the way he took over. He set those eyes on me, and I started shivering inside again.

"I've no time to waste on you," he said. "Make it quick. What's your story?"

"Story?" I said. "Why, simple enough. I'm footloose and roaming for some months, and I get up this way with my pockets about played out. I'm riding by and I see something happening in here, and I drop in to ask a few questions."

"Questions?" he said, pushing his head forward at me. "What kind of questions?"

"Why," I said, "I'm wondering maybe you can tell me, if I push on through these hills, do I come to a town or someplace where maybe I can get a job?"

The three of them stood there staring at me, chewing on this and I sat my saddle staring back, when the bearded man suddenly spoke. "I ain't sure," he said, looking at the roan. "But maybe that's a Rodock horse."

I saw them start to move and I dove sideways off the roan, planning to streak for the brush, and a bullet from the rifle went whipping over the saddle where I'd been, and I hadn't more than bounced the first time when a voice like a chill wind struck the three of them still. "Hold it, and don't move!"

I scrambled up and saw them stiff and frozen, slowly swiveling their necks to look behind them at Rodock and Hugh Claggett and the wicked ready muzzles of their two Henrys.

"Reach," Rodock said, and they reached. "All right, boy. Strip them down."

I cleaned them thoroughly and got, in addition to the rifle and the usual revolvers, two knives from the bearded man and a small but deadly derringer from an inside pocket of the slender man's jacket.

"Got everything?" Rodock said. "Then hobble them good."

I did this just as thoroughly, tying their ankles with about a two-foot stretch between so they could walk short stepped, but not run, and tying their wrists together behind their backs with a loop up and around their necks and down again so that if they tried yanking or pulling they'd be rough on their own Adam's apples.

They didn't like any of this. The slender man didn't say a word, just clamped his mouth and talked hate with his eyes, but the other two started cursing.

"Shut up," Rodock said, "or we'll ram gags down your throats." They shut up, and Rodock motioned to me to set them in a row on the ground leaning against a fallen tree and he hunkered down himself facing them with his Henry across his lap. "Hugh," he said, without looking away from them, "take down those ropes they've been running and bring their horses and any of their stuff you find over here. Ought to be some interesting branding irons about." He took off his hat and set it on the ground beside him. "Hop your horse, boy," he said. "Get over to our hideout and bring everything back here."

When I returned leading our other horses, the three of them were still right in a row leaning against the log and Rodock was still squatted on the ground looking at them. Maybe some words had been passing. I wouldn't know. Anyway, they were all quiet then. The hardcase was staring at his own feet. The bearded man's eyes were roaming around and he had a sick look on his face. The slender man was staring right back at Rodock, and his mouth was only a thin line in his face. Claggett was standing to one side fussing with a rope. I saw he was fixing a hangman's knot on it and had two others already finished and coiled at his feet. When I saw them I had a funny empty feeling under my belt, and I didn't know why. I had seen a hanging before and never felt like that. I guess I had some kind of a queer notion that just hanging those three wouldn't finish the whole thing right. It wouldn't stop me waking at night and thinking about those mares and their crippled hoofs.

My coming seemed to break the silence that had a grip on the whole place. The slender man drew back his lips and spit words at Rodock. "Quit playing games," he said. "Get this over with. We know your reputation."

"Do you?" Rodock said. He stood up and waggled each foot in turn to get the kinks out of his legs. He turned and saw what Claggett was doing, and a strange little mirthless chuckle sounded in his throat. "You're wasting your time, Hugh," he said. "We won't be using those. I'm taking these three in."

Claggett's jaw dropped and his mouth showed open. I guess he was seeing an old familiar pattern broken, and he didn't know how to take it. I wasn't and I had caught something in Rodock's tone. I couldn't have said what it was, but it was sending tingles through my hair roots.

"Don't argue with me, Hugh," Rodock said. "My mind's set. You take some of the food and start hazing the herd toward home. They can do it now if you take them by easy stages. The boy and I'll take these three in."

I helped Claggett get ready and watched him go up the canyon to bunch the herd and get it moving. I turned to Rodock, and he was staring down the back trail.

"Think you could handle four horses on lead ropes, boy?" he said. "The packhorse and their three?"

"Expect I could, strung out," I said. "But why not split them? You take two and I take two."

"I'll be doing something else," he said, and that same little cold chuckle sounded in his throat. "How far do you make it, boy, to the settlement and Kern's office?"

"Straight to it," I said, "I make it close to fifty mile."

"About right," he said. "Kind of a long hike for those used to having horses under them. Hop over and take the hobbles off their feet."

I hopped, but not very fast. I was feeling some disappointed. I was feeling that he was letting me and those mares down. A fifty-mile hike for those three would worry them plenty, and they'd be worrying, too, about what would come at the end of it. Still, it was a disappointment to think about.

"While you're there," Rodock said, "pull their boots off too."

I swung to look at him. He was a big man, as I said before, but I'd run across others that stood taller and filled a doorway more, but right then he was the biggest man I ever saw anywhere anytime in my whole life.

I didn't bother to take off the hobbles. I left them tied so they'd hold the boots together in pairs, and I could hang them flapping over the back of the packhorse. I pulled the boots off, not trying to be gentle, just yanking, and I had a little trouble with the hardcase. He tried to kick me, so I heaved on the rope between his ankles and he came sliding out from the log flat on his back and roughing his bound hands under him, and after that he didn't try anything more. But what I remember best about the three of them then is the yellow of the socks the slender man wore. Those on the others were the usual dark gray, but his were bright yellow. I've thought about them lots of times and never been able to figure why and where he ever got them.

Rodock was rummaging in their stuff that Claggett had collected. He tossed a couple of branding irons toward me. "Bring these along," he said. "Maybe Kern will be interested in them." He picked up a whip, an old but serviceable one with a ten-foot lash, and tested it with a sharp crack. "Get up," he said to the three, and they got up. "I'll be right behind you with this. You'll stay bunched and step right along. Start walking."

They started, and he tucked his Henry in his saddle scabbard and swung up on the bay.

By the time I had the other horses pegged in a line with the packhorse as an anchor at the end and was ready to follow they were heading out of the canyon and I hurried to catch up. I had to get out of the way, too, because Claggett had the herd gathered and was beginning to push the mares along with the foals skittering around through the bushes. Anyone standing on the canyon edge looking down would have seen a queer sight, maybe the damndest procession that ever paraded through that lonesome country. Those three were out in front, walking and putting their feet down careful even in the grass to avoid pebbles and bits of deadwood, with Rodock big and straight on his bay behind them, then me with my string of three saddled but riderless horses and the packhorse, and behind us all the mares and the skittering foals with Claggett weaving on his sorrel to keep the stragglers on the move.

Once out of the canyon we had to separate. Claggett and I had to swing the herd toward the northeast to head for the home range. He had his trouble with the mares because they wanted to follow me and my string. But he and his sorrel knew their business and by hard work made the break and held it. I guess he was a bit huffy about the whole thing because I waved when the distance was getting long between us, and he saw me wave and didn't even raise an arm. I don't know as I blame him for that.

This was midafternoon, and by camping time we had gone maybe ten miles and had shaken down to a steady grind. My horses had bothered the roan some by holding back on the rope and had bothered themselves a few times by spread-eagling and trying to go in different directions, but by now the idea had soaked in and they were plugging along single file and holding their places. The three men out in front had learned to keep moving or feel the whip. The slender man stepped along without paying attention to the other two and never looked back at Rodock and never said a word. The bearded man had found that shouting and cursing simply wore out his throat and had no effect on the grim figure pacing behind them. The hardcase had tried a break, ducking quick to one side and running fast as he could, but Rodock had jumped the bay and headed him the same as you do a steer, and being awkward with his hands tied he had taken a nasty tumble. Not a one of them was going to try that again. Their feet were too tender for hard running anyway, especially out there in the open where the grass was bunchy with bare spaces aplenty, and there were stretches with a kind of coarse gravel underfoot. When Rodock called a halt by water, they were ready to flop on the ground immediately and hitch around and dabble their feet in the stream, and I noticed that the bottoms of their socks were about gone and the soles of their feet were red where they showed in splotches through the dirt ground in. I enjoyed those ten miles, not with a feeling of fun, but with a sort of slow, steady satisfaction.

I prepared food and Rodock and I ate, and then we fed them, one at a time. Rodock sat watch with his Henry on his lap while I untied them and let them eat and wash up a bit and tied them again. We pegged each of them to a tree for the night, sitting on the ground with his back to the trunk and a rope around so he wouldn't topple when he slept. I was asleep almost as soon as I stretched out, and I slept good, and I think Rodock did too.

The next day was more of the same except that we were at it a lot longer, morning and afternoon, and our pace slowed considerably as the day wore on. They were hard to get started again after a noon stop, and the last hours before we stopped they were beginning to limp badly. They weren't thinking anymore of how to make a break. They were concentrating on finding the easiest spots on which to set each step. I figured we covered twenty miles, and I got satisfaction out of every one of them. But the best were in the morning because along late in the afternoon I began to feel tired, not tired in my muscles but tired and somehow kind of shrinking inside. When we stopped, I saw that their socks were just shredded yarn around their ankles and their feet were swelling and angry red and blistery through the dirt. With them sullen and silent and Rodock gray and grim and never wasting a word, I began to feel lonesome, and I couldn't go to sleep right away and found myself checking and rechecking in my mind how far we had come and how many miles we still had to go.

The day after that we started late because there was rain during the night, and we waited till the morning mists cleared. The dampness in the ground must have felt better to their feet for a while because they went along fairly good the first of the morning after we got under way. They were really hard to get started, though, after the noon stop. During the afternoon they went slower and slower, and Rodock had to get mean with the whip around the heels of the hardcase and the bearded man. Not the slender one. That one kept his head high and marched along, and you could tell he was fighting not to wince with every step. After a while, watching him, I began to get the feel of him. He was determined not to give us the satisfaction of seeing this get to him in any serious way. I found myself watching him too much, too closely, so I dropped behind a little more, tagging along in the rear with my string, and before Rodock called the halt by another stream, I began to see the occasional small red splotches in the footprints on dusty stretches that showed the blisters on their feet were breaking.

The best I could figure we had come maybe another ten miles during the day, the last few mighty slow. That made about forty all together, and when I went over it in my mind I had to call it twelve more to go because we had curved off the most direct route some to avoid passing near a couple of line cabins of the only other ranch in that general neighborhood north of the settlement.

There weren't many words in any of us as we went

through the eating routine. I didn't know men's faces were capable of such intense hatred as showed plain on the hardcase and the bearded man. They gobbled their food and glared at Rodock from their night posts against trees, and for all I know glared without stopping all night because they had the same look the next morning. It was the slender man who suddenly took to talking. The hatred he'd had at the start seemed to have burned away. What was left was a kind of hard pride that kept his eyes alive. He looked up from his food at Rodock.

"It was a good try," he said.

"It was," Rodock said. "But not good enough. Your mistake was hurting my horses."

"I had to," the man said. "That was part of it. I saw some of your horses on a stage line once. I had to have a few."

"If you wanted some of my horses," Rodock said, "why didn't you come and buy them?"

"I was broke," the man said.

"You were greedy," Rodock said. "You had to take all in that basin. If you'd cut out a few and kept on going, you might have made it."

"Maybe," the man said. "Neither of us will ever know now. You planning to keep this up all the way in?"

"I am," Rodock said.

"Then turn us over?" the man said.

"Yes," Rodock said.

"You're the one that's greedy," the man said.

He shut up and finished his food and crawled to his tree and refused to look at Rodock again. I fixed his rope, and then I had trouble getting to sleep. I lay a long time before I dozed and what sleep I got wasn't much good.

In the morning Rodock was grayer and grimmer than ever before. Maybe he hadn't slept much either. He stood off by himself and let me do everything alone. I couldn't make the hardcase and the bearded man get on their feet, and I found my temper mighty short and was working up a real mad when the slender man, who was up and ready, stepped over and kicked them, kicked them with his own swollen feet that had the remains of his yellow socks flapping around the ankles.

"Get up!" he said. "Damn you, get up! We're going through with this right!"

They seemed a lot more afraid of him than of me. They staggered up and they stepped along with him as Rodock came close with the whip in his hand, and we got our pathetic parade started again. We couldn't have been moving much more than a mile an hour, and even that pace slowed, dropping to about a crawl when we hit rough stretches, and more and more red began to show in the footprints. And still that slender man marched along, slow but dogged, the muscles in his neck taut as he tried to stay straight without wincing.

Rodock was mean and nasty, crowding close behind them, using the whip to raise the dust around the lagging two. I didn't like the look of him. The skin of his face was stretched too tight and his eyes were too deep sunk. I tried riding near him and making a few remarks to calm him, but he snapped at me like I might be a horse thief myself, so I dropped behind and stayed there.

He didn't stop at noontime, but kept them creeping along, maybe because he was afraid he'd never get them started again. It was only a short while after that the bearded man fell down, just crumpled and went over sideways and lay still. It wasn't exactly a faint or anything quite like that. I think he had cracked inside, had run out his score and quit trying, even trying to stay conscious. He was breathing all right, but it was plain he wouldn't do any more walking for a spell.

Rodock sat on his horse and looked down at him. "All right, boy," he said. "Hoist him on one of your string, and tie him so he'll stay put." I heaved him on the first of the horses behind me and slipped a rope around the horse's barrel to hold him. Rodock sat on his bay and looked at the other two men, not quite sure what to do, and the slender one stared back at him, contempt sharp on his face, and Rodock shook out the whip. "Get moving, you two!" he said, and we started creeping along again.

It was about another hour and maybe another mile when the hardcase began screaming. He threw himself on the ground and rolled and thrashed and kept screaming, then stretched out taut and suddenly went limp all over, wide awake and conscious, but staring up as if he couldn't focus on anything around him.

Rodock had to stop again, chewing his lower lip and frowning. "All right, boy," he said. "Hoist that one too." I did, the same as the other one, and when I looked around damned if that slender man wasn't walking on quite a distance ahead with Rodock right behind him.

I didn't want to watch, but I couldn't help watching that man stagger on. I think he had almost forgotten us. He was intent on the terrible task of putting one foot forward after the other and easing his weight onto it. Rodock, bunched on his bay and staring at him, was the one who cracked first. The sun was still up the sky, but he shouted a halt and when the man kept going he had to jump down and run ahead and grab him.

It was a grim business making camp. The other two had straightened out some but they had no more spirit in them than a pair of limp rabbits. I had to lift them down, and it wasn't until they had some food in them that they began to perk up at all. They seemed grateful when I hiked a ways and brought water in a folding canvas bucket from one of the packs and let them take turns soaking their swollen bloody feet in it. Then I took a saddle blanket and ripped it in pieces and wrapped some of them around their feet. I think I did that so I wouldn't find myself always sneaking looks at their feet. I did the same for the slender man, and all the time I was doing it he looked at me with that contempt on his face, and I didn't give a damn. I did this even though I thought Rodock might not like it, but he didn't say a word. I noticed he wouldn't look at me, and I found I didn't want to look at him either. I tried to keep my mind busy figuring how far we had come and made it six miles with six more still to go, and I was wishing those six would fade away and the whole thing would be over. The sleep I got that night wasn't worth anything to me.

In the morning I didn't want any breakfast, and I wasn't going to prepare any unless Rodock kicked me into it. He was up ahead of me, standing quiet and chewing his lower lip and looking very old and very tired, and he didn't say a word to me. I saddled the horses the way I had been every morning, because that was the easiest way to tote the saddles along and tied them to the usual string. The slender man was awake, watching me, and by the time I finished the other two were too. They were thoroughly beaten. They couldn't have walked a quarter of a mile with the devil himself herding them.

I thought to hell with Rodock and led the horses up close and hoisted the two, with them quick to help, into their saddles. They couldn't put their feet in the stirrups, but they could sit the saddles and let their feet dangle. I went over to the slender man and started to take hold of him and he glared at me and shook himself free of my hands and twisted around and strained till he was up on his feet. I stood there gaping at him, and he hobbled away, heading straight for the settlement. I couldn't move. I was sort of frozen inside watching him. He made about fifty yards and his legs buckled under him. The pain in his feet must have been stabbing up with every step, and he simply couldn't stand any longer. And then while I stared at him he started crawling on his hands and knees.

"God damn it, boy!" Rodock's voice behind me made me jump. "Grab that man! Haul him back here!"

I ran and grabbed him and after the first grab, he didn't fight and I hauled him back. "Hoist him on his horse," Rodock said, and I did that. And then Rodock started cursing. He cursed that man and he cursed me and then he worked back over us both again. He wasn't a cursing man and he didn't know many words and he didn't have much imagination at it, but what he did know he used over and over again and after a while he ran down and stopped and chewed his lower lip. He turned and stalked to the packhorse and took the pairs of tied boots and came along the line tossing each pair over the withers of the right horse. He went back to the packs and pulled out the weapons I'd found on the three and checked to see that the guns were empty and shook the last of the

flour out of its bag and put the weapons in it with the
rifle barrel sticking out the top. He tied the bag to the
pommel of the slender man's saddle.

"All right, boy," he said. "Take off those lead ropes
and untie their hands."

When I had done this and they were rubbing their
wrists, he stepped close to the slender man's horse and
spoke up at the man. "Back to the last creek we passed
yesterday," he said, "and left along it a few miles you
come to Shirttail Fussel's shack. From what I hear for a
price he'll hide out anything and keep his mouth shut.
A man with sense would fix his feet there and keep traveling and stay away from this range the rest of his days."

The slender man didn't say a word. He pulled his horse
around and started in the direction of the creek and the
other two tagged him, and what I remember is that look
of hard pride still in his eyes, plain and sharp against the
pinched and strained bleakness of his face.

We watched them go and I turned to Rodock. He was
old, older even than I thought he was when I first saw him,
and tired with heavy circles under his eyes. At that moment, I didn't like him at all, not because he had let them
go, but because of what he had put me through, and it
was my turn to curse him. I did it right. I did a better job
than he had done before, and he never even wagged a
muscle.

"Shut up," he said finally. "I need a drink." He went
to his bay and mounted and headed for the settlement. I
watched him, hunched forward and old in the saddle, and
I was ashamed. I took the lead rope of the packhorse and
climbed on the roan and followed him. I was glad when

he put the bay into a fast trot because I was fed up with sitting on a walking horse.

He bobbed along ahead of me, a tired old man who seemed too small for that big bay, and then a strange thing began to happen. He began to sit straighter in the saddle and stretch up and look younger by the minute, and when we reached the road and headed into the settlement he was Jeremy Rodock riding straight and true on a Rodock horse and riding it like it was the part of him that in a way it really was. He hit a good clip the last stretch, and my roan and the packhorse were seesawing on the lead rope trying to keep up when we reached the buildings and pulled in by a tie rail. I swung down right after him and stepped up beside him, and we went toward the saloon. We passed the front window of Kern's office, and he was inside and came popping out.

"Hey, you two," he said. "Anything to report?"

We stopped and faced him, and he looked at us kind of funny. I guess we did look queer, dirty and unshaved and worn in spots.

"Not a thing," Rodock said. "I told you we could be taking a camp trip and that's all I'll say. Except that I'm not missing any stock and haven't stretched any rope."

We went into the saloon and to the bar and downed a stiff one apiece.

"Mister Rodock," I said, "when you think about it, that man beat us."

"Damned if he didn't," Rodock said. He didn't seem to be bothered by it and I know I wasn't. "Listen to me, Son," he said. "I expect I haven't been too easy to get along with for quite a few weeks lately. I want you to know I've noticed how you and that roan have stuck to my heels over some mighty rough trail. Now we've got to get home and get a horse ranch moving again. We'll be needing some hands. Come along with me, Son, and we'll look around. I'd like your opinion on them before hiring any."

That was Jeremy Rodock. They don't grow men like that around here anymore.

ABOUT THE AUTHOR

Phyllis R. Fenner was born in Almond, New York, and for thirty-two years was the librarian of the Plandome Road School in Manhasset, New York. In 1955 she retired and made her permanent home in Manchester, Vermont. She holds degrees from Mount Holyoke College and from the Columbia Library School, and has traveled extensively throughout this country, Canada, Mexico, and Europe.

Miss Fenner's work has brought her in touch with library schools throughout the country; she has also done book reviewing, given lectures about children's books, and held story hours for children. In addition, she is widely known for her many distinguished anthologies.